Stay In My Swamp

An Ogre Happily Ever After

G.M. Fairy

G.M. Fairy

Copyright © 2023 by G.M. Fairy

FIRST EDITION

To all the monsters that deserve a happily ever after.

Please Note

This book is the second part of a two-book series. In order for the characters and events of this book to make sense, you must read the first book, *Get In My Swamp: An Ogre Love Story*.

Content Warning

For a full list of content warnings in this book, please go to my Instagram @g.m.fairyauthor and check the Google Docs in the link in my bio.

Contents

CHAPTER ONE

Liona

"Ah fuck!" I smack my cheek and brush my hair off my face. "There are bugs everywhere!"

Beck sighs as he scoops jam out of a glass jar and spreads it across his toast. "I don't know if you realized this, but we live in a swamp, and there tends to be bugs around."

I glare at him. "Very funny, smart ass." I know I'm being a bitch. Beck has gone above and beyond to put together this picnic as a romantic gesture. He set up a checkered blanket beneath a wide oak tree. He made sourdough bread, goat cheese, jam, and freshly squeezed lemonade. He even picked a bouquet and placed them in the center of his spread. I know I should be *drooling* over his dick right now, but I've just not been myself lately. I'm sore, I'm cranky, and I'm *starving*. Like man-eating ogre starving. I just can't control my temper.

Of course, I know why I'm on edge. The letter I just received from Mr. Pigeon, the magical community's mailman from the outside world, burns a hole in my pocket, searing all my focus.

I grab the other knife, scoop a colossal dollop of jam onto my piece of bread, and push it into my mouth, not even caring that there are probably crumbs all over my white tank top or strawberry guts smeared across my face. The bitch is hangry, and I think Beck and I will benefit if I feed my beast as quickly as possible. I feel like a dick for not telling Beck about the letters, but I think it's better for everyone if I keep it to myself. And eat.

"You have jam all over your face." Beck laughs and motions to his lips. He's wearing a cream linen shirt with only the bottom two buttons fastened, revealing his muscular torso. His brown hair blows in the breeze.

I freeze, glaring at him. I lower my toast to my plate in front of me, not breaking my gaze.

Beck's smile fades as he stares at me.

I don't know what's come over me, but I've had the sudden urge to be...*naughty*, but honestly, what's new?

In a snap, I stick my fingers into the jam and smear it across Beck's green face. I grin at him on all fours, my breast almost pressing against him. "Now you have jam on your face too." My heart pounds as I watch his expression.

When I first saw Beck after falling into his trap almost a year ago, I thought he was the most terrifying ogre I'd ever seen. He's seven feet tall, bulging with muscles, green, and constantly looks like he wants to gobble me up. It didn't take long for me to swoon over his harsh features and *want* him to devour every inch of me.

I'm never frightened of him. I know he would die before he let anything harm me, but of course, there's always a dark side of him – the monster within. Some might think I have a death wish, but I *love* poking the bear just to see how far he'll take his predatory instincts. Plus, I love being a brat. Like Beck always says, "Bad girls get tied up and fucked," as if it's a warning. He sure as hell knows that being bound and completely stuffed must be one of my favorite things.

His body stiffens and his breathing slows. His eyes darken, a fire blazing behind them.

I look down at his fists, clenched by his side. I make a small gasp, anticipating what comes next. Neither of us moves, each waiting to see what happens, except I know how this ends.

I count to three in my head before popping up to my feet and darting toward the woods. I'm not wearing shoes, but I don't let that slow me down. I look behind me when I don't immediately hear Beck barreling after me, but it only takes a few seconds before his thunderous footsteps echo through the forest. He gave me a head start—that cheeky bastard.

I push away the tree limbs and brush in my path. My heart pounds out of my chest. There are two sides of me, one that wants to get away, that's sure he will consume.

The other that *needs* him to catch me and hopes he grabs and holds me down as he has his way with me.

He's getting closer. His finger brushes against my shoulder as he reaches for me, but he stumbles a bit and I'm able to propel myself just a little farther in front of him. My lead is only granted for a few more seconds before his powerful arms wrap around me, and he brings me to the ground. He manages to throw himself under me before I hit the ground so that I fall on top of him.

He holds me close to him, but I use all my force, trying to pull out of his grasp. He chuckles and shakes his head before flipping me over so I'm lying on the forest floor, and he's holding my arms down with his body hovering over mine. He sighs, "Really, Liona? We're playing this game again?"

I struggle against his grip. "I don't know what you're talking about," I grunt, straining. "You scared me."

He sighs again but with a wicked smile plastered on his face. "I'm wearing my nice shirt, and now look at you; you're filthy."

"I thought you were going to eat me." I try to use my legs to kick him away, but he's too fast for me and holds my legs down with him. I'm immobilized, wholly restrained by his will. My body slacks, accepting defeat, anticipating the delicious punishment already making my insides heat.

His eyes darken. All practical reason about the state of our clothing evaporates from him. He runs his tongue over his fangs. "Oh, I'm going to eat you alright, but you've been a bad girl, so now you'll be punished first." He transfers his grip of my arms above my head to one hand and uses his free one to rip my tank top off my body.

The wind tickles my already sensitive breasts.

He leans down to my ear. "Don't you look delicious." His tongue trails from my earlobe down my neck, and a moan escapes from my lips. He travels lower and lower until he laps at one of my nipples.

The build-up of the chase and now the sweet friction of his rough tongue is almost too much for me. I cry out in ecstasy. You would think that after nearly a year of exploring each other's bodies in every way possible, I wouldn't react this way to him anymore. I'm pretty sure we could fuck for two lifetimes' worth, and I would never grow tired of his tongue on my tits or my cunt or anywhere else he chooses. Every time we come together, it's electric. It's a drug I can't get enough of.

After only a few circles around my nipple, he stops, pulling away from me but still holding my arms above my head.

I gasp as if in pain. The absence of his rock-hard body chills me. I want him back against me, his tongue dragging against my most sensitive spots. But he just stares down at me with a hungry but commanding look.

"Come back," I whisper with urgency.

"I don't think so. You need to be punished, and I love watching you squirm under my grip."

I swallow.

With his free hand, Beck reaches into his pants and pulls out his cock, already hard and dripping with pre-cum.

The sight of it makes my mouth water. "Please," I beg. I want him inside of me. However he sees fit.

"Patient, little one. You'll watch me stroke my cock until you beg me to fuck you."

I don't know how long I can last. My body bucks, trying to rub myself against him, but the pressure on my wrists and lower half doesn't waver, even as he strokes himself, slow and steady, keeping his gaze on me.

His head falls back, and he closes his eyes as if he almost can't control himself. "You look so delicious when you're helpless. I can barely take it."

He dips down again, rubbing his body against mine. "Yes!" I cry.

His dick rubs against my thigh as he devours my mouth. He lets go of my wrists. One of his hands cups the back of my neck while the other trails down my body, lower and lower, until... "God, you're wet. You're ready for me. Good girl." He traces the outside of my core, teasing me even more. He dips one giant finger inside of me. "Oh God, you're still so tight." I'm unsure if my body will ever get completely used to his size. I love it, but getting ready to take him takes a bit. Monster dicks have consequences, but I'll take being sore as a trade for being so completely filled.

He dips in another finger, pulling in and out.

"That's so good," I moan. "I need more."

He growls. "Aren't you a greedy one? Luckily, you caught me in a good mood." He pulls his fingers out of me and positions himself at my entrance. He holds me still even while I try to slide down and impale myself on him. He's more concerned about my well-being than I am. What a shame.

He slowly eases himself in with small movements, stretching me to my limit.

I wrap my legs around his hips, eager for more of him, all of him.

He finally loses control, pounding his entire length into me, hitting that perfect spot with every thrust. "Fuck!" he moans. "You're taking me so good. Your pussy was made for me." This is one of his favorite sentiments. He thoroughly believes that we were pre-destined for each other, and it's hard to deny. I fit around him so perfectly, not just physically, but my entire essence.

Our cries synchronize as my body tightens around him. I'm dizzy from the pleasure, the size of him, the sheer force pounding into me with such strength. My body welcomes it, and my nerves turn into a warm rush of molten lava. Everything in me explodes at the same time. Beck gives one last cry, spilling into me until I feel it pool underneath me.

He pulls back and looks down, out of breath. "So much come for such a little body to take." He falls next to me, pulls me in his arms, and kisses me on my forehead.

I roll over and nuzzle into his side, trying to ignore the strange rumble in my stomach. "Your body knows I'll only be satisfied when you completely fill me."

He chuckles and then strokes my hair as I lie on his chest, a comfortable silence falling over us.

I close my eyes, fully surrendering myself to this moment. I still feel guilty for having such a bad attitude during his picnic. In fact, I feel a little queasy. I guess that's what I get for skipping a meal to get fucked in the forest.

"I'm sorry for ruining your picnic. I know you spent a lot of time planning it. I've just been in a bad mood lately."

Beck kisses the top of my head. "It's okay. I think this was much more fun than what I had planned anyway."

"Even if I got us all dirty and ruined our clothes?"

"Especially."

I cuddle closer against him. "I love you," I sigh sleepily.

"Speaking of that." He sits up, and I pull back, offended he would ruin such a comfortable moment. "There's something I want to ask you." He reaches over to his pants next to him and pulls something out of his pocket. He flips open a black velvet box and reveals a ring with a light green, emerald the size of a dime, encircled with intricate gold vines.

Oh no. My stomach gurgles.

He gets up to his knees and scoots closer to me, eyes full of love and tenderness. "I planned to ask you this during the picnic, but this does seem more... us." He takes a deep breath. "Liona, I love you and want to be a part of you in every way possible. I want to be your lover, best friend, ogre, and husband. Will you marry me?"

The world spins around me. It's like the universe is playing a cruel joke on me. Of course, the marriage question would come up now. The guilt of keeping the letters a secret hits me like a ton of bricks, sending another jolt of pain to my stomach. I don't know what to say. All my thoughts are a tangled mess, and so much feeling is flooding through me. I feel like I might explode. No, wait. I definitely am going to explode. Everything is coming up.

I bend over and vomit my guts out.

CHAPTER TWO

Beck

Just as every man imagines, he meets the girl of his dreams, falls in love, orchestrates a beautiful engagement, and she vomits right when he pops the big question. Perfect.

But what more could I expect? Liona and I's relationship has always been somewhat unconventional (starting with me trapping her in a cage). How could I think our engagement would carry on without any road bumps? I try not to let it get to me as I rush around our cottage, preparing a bowl of chicken broth for her. She's vomited a few more times since we made it back inside, and now she's curled up in our bed, making moaning sounds, and not in a good way. She must have a stomach bug or something. She definitely didn't vomit because the thought of spending the rest of her life with a green, ugly ogre was so disgusting. Definitely not.

I shake the self-doubt out of my head and run to her side, the weight of the engagement ring in my pocket slapping against my side with every step. "Liona, you need to eat something." I place the bowl on the bedside table.

She's lying down, her full eyelashes fanning her closed eyes. I managed to clean the dirt off her from our romp in the wood, and even though her skin is sickly pale, her internal glow still radiates. Her chocolate brown hair frames her head. She's so damn beautiful, even when she's ill.

She groans, pulling a pillow over her face. "No. No food."

"It's just chicken broth. If you throw up again, I'll get you something else. You won't feel better until you regain your strength and some calories."

She sighs and pushes herself up, letting me know she agrees to my offering.

I carefully place the soup in her hands, and she feeds herself slowly.

I chuckle. "Do you feel any better?" I sit at the edge of the bed by her feet, supporting myself with my out-stretched arm.

She takes one last slurp of the broth and brings it down to her lap. "A little. I think the vomiting got almost every-thing out."

"Good." I give her a weak smile. I wonder which of us will bring up what happened first. It should be her. She's the one that didn't answer my question, even if she was interrupted by vomiting. She's not sick enough to claim she forgot what happened. I know she heard my question.

I had been dreaming about asking Liona to marry me for months. In the magical community, marriage isn't as necessary as it seems the human world makes it, but it's still something that we do. I never thought I would be the type of ogre to care about such silly things as proclaiming my love to a room full of people or signing a legal document of our commitment, but Liona brings out a different side of me. If there's anything in this world that Liona and I can do together, if there's a way we can be ever more committed to each other, I want to do it. I want everything with her. Everything that two people can give to each other.

The ring still in my pocket is a family heirloom. It's one of the last things that I kept of my mother. Of course, I had to get the ring resized to fit Liona's tiny human fingers. Winston the Wizard helped with this using some magic. I didn't get to tell this to Liona yet, but I figured it would come up after she said yes, embraced me, and then sucked my dick to reveal her joy further. Obviously, the plan of events took a turn.

After a few seconds of silence, I sigh, realizing I'm the one that must bring up the proposal. My heart aches that she's not more excited about it and from the anticipation that she will hurt me even more. "We should probably talk."

She looks down at her soup, twirling her spoon around in the leftover broth but not trying to eat more. "I don't know. I don't think I'm well enough to talk much." Her cheeks flush.

I can tell she's lying, but what more can I do? At this point, if I insist that she gives me an answer, I know it won't be yes. "Okay." I nod, trying to hide my hurt but knowing I'm probably failing. I stand up and take the bowl away from her.

Her eyes catch mine, and she searches my face. She looks like she wants to comfort me, but I turn away and walk toward the kitchen.

As I wash her bowl in the sink, she pulls the covers off her and shuffles over to me. Her arms wrap around my lower half, and she rests her head on my back. "I'm sorry, Beck. I know I ruined everything." I'm unsure if she means the picnic, the proposal, or us. I feel her body shake slightly as if she's crying. "I love you. So much," she whispers.

I turn to face her, wrap my arms around her, and rub her back.

She pulls her face away from my chest and looks up at me, her eyes big and full of tears.

I lean down and give her a soft kiss.

She grabs my neck, pulls me into her, and lifts herself, wrapping her legs around me.

I grab her bottom and walk to bed, not breaking our kiss. I lie down with her; our kisses are soft but full of need. I don't care that she just threw up. I don't care that she didn't accept my proposal. All I want is her forever; if this is how it has to be, I can live with that. As long as I have her.

CHAPTER THREE

Liona

"Don't be a little bitch, Liona. Stop crying," I whisper to myself as I dart around the house, trying to stay focused on the task at hand.

Beck is hunting for deer, but I know he'll return soon. I'm unsure why I feel like I need to get this done before he returns. Probably because I know I'll never get it done with his presence near me. He'll understand once I explain everything to him when I come back. I know how he'll react if I tell him about the letters I've been getting. He'll want to take it into his own hands and probably murder someone. Although I don't mind (the prick deserves it), it would put him and everyone in the community at risk. I can't let that happen.

It's been two days since Beck asked me to marry him. We haven't brought it up since then, thank God, but I can see the pain in his face at the edge of every smile. I can't bring myself to say yes to Beck's proposal right before I do what I'm about to do. The third letter just came this morning—this one with a threat. I need to take action into my own hands. I pick up the letter from the counter one more time. "Come to LA or else...." Yep. It's still a threat, complete with pictures. Not even blurry pictures, crisp HD photos. How could we have been so stupid?

I love my life here at the swamp. The magical community finally accepts me as one of their own. Sure, there are some creatures I do my best to avoid (some people never change), but I have my own life here. I help Beck with gardening. I socialize with the fairies at the coffee shop in town. I volunteer at the local school by reading to the children. Although my life is quieter and slow, I've never been happier. Of course, Beck is the reason for most of my happiness, and it pains me that I'm the root of his most recent pain.

I jolt when the front door slams, bringing my hands up from my suitcase.

Beck's eyes catch mine. I'm sure he can read the guilt on my face because he doesn't make any sudden movements as he scans our cottage, the evidence of my packing from the open closets and drawers. "What's going on?" he asks, pain and panic already at the edge of his voice.

My heart beats out of my chest as I leave my almost packed suitcase and walk towards him. "Beck, I need to get away for a little while."

"Okay...but why?" He keeps his eyes glued to me, not moving away from the door.

I can't help it. I'm a little bitch. The tears I willed to stay back flow out of me, running down my cheeks. I rush towards him, burying my head in his chest, the sweet smell of his musk meeting my nostrils, already making me homesick. "I'm so sorry, but I just have to go."

"Liona." Beck hunches down and pulls me back to look me in the eyes. "What's wrong?"

"There are just some things I need to take care of back in LA. I promise everything will go back to normal when I come back." I look up at him. His eyes are pools of misery.

"When are you coming back?"

"I'm not sure. I don't know how long this is going to take. Probably just a week or two."

He nods and looks ahead as if accepting that he's lost me.

I pull back from him and rush to the kitchen table. "But I'm staying at the Beverly Place Hotel. You can call me there." I pick up my old cell phone from the table I brought from LA. I've never had a reason to use it, and it's stayed dead in a drawer. I've been charging it while Beck was hunting. I kept it because I knew it might come in handy at some point. I just never thought it would be because I was leaving, and Beck needed a way to reach me. I walk over to him and place it in his hand.

He just stares down at it. I'd thought that offering a way to reach me would make my leaving easier for him, but that doesn't seem to be the case.

I wrap my arms around him again. "Beck, I love you. I really do. I'm not leaving because of anything you've done. I just need to figure my shit out."

He rests his free hand on the back of my head, and I listen to his heartbeat, soaking it in. After a moment of silence, he speaks. "We don't have to get married if you don't want to."

Tears rush down my cheeks again. I hate that I'm hurting him this much. Of course, he thinks I'm running away because I don't want to marry him. "Beck, this is just too complicated. I rather explain everything to you when I have things figured out." I know I should just tell him and let him help me solve this, but I'm embarrassed and don't think I'd like how he chooses to deal with this. I need to do this on my own.

"Okay," he says, defeated.

"I love you." I hold on tighter and then pull back.

"I love you more than you know," he says as he walks back out the door.

CHAPTER FOUR

Beck

It's only been a day since Liona left, but I'm unsure how long I can last. I've lived most of my life in solitude, so I had an inkling of hope that Liona's absence would be easier to bear. But I'd grown used to her presence, her laugh, her smile, the feel of her velvety hair, and the way she fit so perfectly around my cock. The last two days have felt like I'm not really alive, just wandering in some in-between world.

I'm lying in bed, unable to sleep. The phone Liona gave me burns in my hand. She called me the minute she made it to her hotel. She was already crying and telling me how much she missed me when she heard my voice. I'm not used to Liona crying so much. She's not usually the kind of person for so many emotions. It scares me. I worry about whatever she's dealing with. It must be difficult and I hate that she has to do whatever she's doing on her own. I'm not sure how much longer I can take waiting for her. It's not that I don't trust her. I just don't want her to deal with anything so difficult without me. We're partners; we're supposed to be there for each other. What can be so great that I can't help her with?

A part of me can't shake the feeling that she left because of me. I know that she loves me. Well, I used to know she loved me, but now it feels like I drove her away. She doesn't want to get married and can't stand being around me. I've experienced her love on a spiritual level, but maybe her love has an expiration date. One that was sped up by the thought of being with me forever.

I can't continue to wrestle with my doubts, so I call her. It's late in LA too, and I don't want to worry her, but I can't help the aching need to hear her voice.

I type in the hotel's phone number and the extension to her room. The phone rings only three times. "Hello?" Her voice is sleepy but full of worry.

"Hi, it's me."

"Is everything okay?"

"Yeah, I just can't sleep. I miss you."

She's silent for a moment as if collecting herself. "I miss you too. I'm not sleeping that great, either." I don't know why this comforts me, but it's nice to know that she's struggling without me. Maybe if it gets too bad, she'll just come back home. Maybe I should remind her just what she's missing. Maybe she's falling out of love with me, but I *know* I can give her enough pleasure for her to stay with me. I just need to remind her of this. "Oh yeah? What do you miss about me most?" I ask in a low growl.

She chuckles as if sensing my game. "Oh, there's so many things."

"Go on," I muse, clutching the sheets beside me.

She sighs. "Well, I do miss your cooking."

"Understandable. I am a superb cook."

"I also miss you picking up after me."

"Oh yes, I'd hate to see the state of your hotel room right now. There's probably clothes everywhere."

"Are you sure about that? Are you sure you don't want to see what's in this room?" Her voice turns airy.

"Well, I'd like to see one thing."

"And what's that?"

"I'd like to see what you're doing right now."

"Oh, you definitely want to see what I'm doing right now."

"And why is that?"

Her voice slows. "I think you'd find my position rather interesting."

"Do share." My heart beats out of my chest. Who knew her words alone, even when she's thousands of miles away, could have this effect on me?

"I'm lying on my bed..."

"What are you wearing?"

"You know me. I don't wear anything to bed."

I groan and bite my knuckles. You'd think after being celibate for most of my life, I could go two days without having or thinking about sex, but for the past year, Liona and I haven't even gone a day without fucking each other. My body needs her. I sit up in bed and pull out my already throbbing cock. The room is dark, only illuminated by the moon outside my window. Liona would look unearthly in this moonlight, sprawled across my white sheets. "God, I wish I was lying next to you."

"Oh yeah?" Her voice is heavy. "And what would you do if you were here?"

"First, I would kiss you."

"But of course. Then what?"

"Then I'd kiss your body."

"Where exactly on my body?"

"I'd start at your tits. I'd flick my tongue back and forth over your hard nipples."

"Yeah?" She gasps.

"Are you touching yourself?" I say as I feel my length, dripping with need.

"Yes," she purrs. "I'm so wet right now. My fingers glide through so easily."

I groan. "I want to taste you."

She moans. "Are you touching yourself?"

"Oh yeah. I'm hard as a rock. My dick begs for you."

"I wish I was on top of you. Sliding up and down your cock. I would slide on so easily. I'm dripping."

I can imagine it so vividly, almost feel her skin beneath my grasp. "Are you fucking yourself with your fingers right now?" My voice is labored, trying to hold back as I slide my hand up and down.

"Yes," she cries. "But I wish it was you fucking me. God, I miss your dick. I wish you were so deep inside me, filling me until I almost break."

"Fuck, Liona. I'm so close. If you were here right now, I would be filling you up already. I know you like it when you're overflowing with me."

"Yes," she cries louder, and I know she's close.

"Tell me what that pretty pussy looks like right now."

"It's begging for you. My fingers are gliding back and forth...."

"I want you to focus on your clit. I want you to come for me."

"Oh God, it's so good. I'm gonna come," she says between gasps.

"Yes, come for me, baby. We'll come together."

We both cry out in pure ecstasy. Even when we're hundreds of miles away, we can time up our orgasms at the exact same moment. Our bodies were made for each other.

A moment of silence passes between us as we catch our breath. The aching need for her washes over me immediately after the wave of my pleasure passes through. "Liona, I miss you. Please come home."

She's quiet for a moment, but then, in a voice filled with tears, she says, "I miss you too. It's just...."

I can't take it anymore. "Liona, can't you just tell me what's going on? Maybe I can help."

"That's what I'm worried about."

"What do you mean?"

She sighs. "I'm worried that you'll try to help and get yourself or other people hurt."

"Liona, I promise I'll do whatever you want me to do. Just tell me what's going on." My mind fills with thoughts of Liona with a secret family or that she's discovered some chronic illness.

She's silent for a moment as if considering. "Okay," she finally says. "But you have to promise you can't come to me. It will just make everything worse."

"I promise," I say, crossing my fingers.

"About two weeks ago, I got a letter from Lawrence."

My heart stops.

"He knows where we live."

"Shit."

"Shit indeed." She sighs and continues. "Apparently, his father just died and in his will, there's a stipulation that he must be married in order to claim his full inheritance."

"So he wants to marry you?" I jump out of bed, about to charge out the door and get her.

"Yes."

"Liona, is that what you're doing in LA? You're marrying Lawrence? Why?" I'm crushed, but anger at Lawrence rushes through me.

"He's blackmailing me. Blackmailing us. When you came to get me in LA in your disguise, they got pictures of you. Lawrence owns half of the security cameras in LA. He hired someone to follow us back to the swamp, so he knows where we live. He knows about the magical community. If I don't marry him, he'll leak the pictures and the location. Everyone is in danger."

"How do you know he won't just leak the pictures even if you marry him?"

She sighs angrily. "I don't! But what can I do? This is my best chance at saving the community. I can't even threaten him with my blackmail about him and Victoria because I have no proof."

I fling the cottage door open. "That's it. I'm coming to get you. This is bullshit. I'll fucking kill that prick."

"No, Beck, you can't. You are an ogre. Someone will spot you and Lawrence will just have more proof to send out. Your last disguise didn't really fool anyone. We're lucky the news isn't already out."

At this moment, I don't care. I don't care if everyone knows about me and the whole magical community is burned to the ground as long as I have Liona.

"Beck, I know you're fuming right now but it's going to be okay. Lawrence wants me to marry him as a front so he can really be with Victoria." She makes a gagging noise. "I can come back home and never have to see him again after this. It should just take a week."

I can't stand how Lawrence is using her, ruining marriage for her, with blackmail. No wonder she didn't want to say yes to me. How can she be excited about marriage when she's being forced to marry someone else against her will?

"Why does it have to be you?"

"Beck, I'm his best choice. He has something he can hold over me. I'll go away, not ask for any money and leave him and Victoria to their incestual paradise."

"Liona, I know there's a way out of this. I can help." My last plea.

Her voice is soft. "Maybe, but this is the easiest way without anyone getting hurt." She's silent for a moment as if thinking. "Maybe if you can come up with a better disguise, you could..." She stops herself. "No, killing him would be too messy and he probably has the photos and location ready to send out if anything happens to him. He's made it seem that way, at least."

"I can think of something!"

"No, Beck. Stop. You promised. I'm sorry my life is so complicated. I'm sorry I'm about to marry someone else. I feel like the worst person ever, but I do love you so much. I just want to keep you safe and end this part of my life for good."

Even as she says this, I know that won't be the case. Lawrence will always be coming back for more. Wanting more for her. This isn't the end. It's just the beginning. I push my thoughts to the side and say, "I know, Liona. I love you too."

She breathes out as if relieved that I'm finally accepting her plan.

"It's late," I say. "Why don't you try to go to bed?"

"Yeah, okay. I love you." Her voice sounds tired and teary.

"I love you too."

I hang up the phone. My brain schemes my next plan. I'm sure as shit not letting Liona handle this alone. I'm fixing it and I know just the person who can help me.

CHAPTER FIVE

Beck

I use the old brass knocker to pound on the circular door three times. The house looks like all the other wizards' houses in the village, a quaint stone cottage surrounded by well-kept greenery. A pile of smoke trails from the chimney, and the smell of herbs seeps from the walls.

The door cracks and a dark curly mop pokes out. "Beck? What are you doing here so late?" Winston cleans his circular glasses and puts them back on the bridge of his nose.

"Hey, Winston. Nice to see you too." I push myself in, with no time for formalities, glancing around and freezing once I see the inside of his home. It's nothing like I expected. There is nothing old or withering. There are no cauldrons full of bubbling liquid or black cats lounging on every surface. Something darts past my feet. Okay, maybe there's one black cat.

"Nice place you got here. I can't say I was expecting it to be so..."

"Modern?" Winston finishes.

I nod.

He glares at me with tired eyes, his arms crossed over his chest. "So, Beck, what do I owe this pleasure at four in the morning?"

"I need a disguise."

"A disguise?"

"Yes, I need you to make me look less like an ogre."

Winston walks over and pats me on the shoulder. "Ah, buddy, don't let those gnomes get to you. You aren't that ugly. Besides, you have Liona."

"What? No." Frankly, I should be pissed that the gnomes are talking shit about me, but I don't give a fuck. "I need the disguise for Liona. I need to rescue her."

"Rescue her? From what?"

I'm about to reveal everything that's happened with Liona, but I stop. Winston has a lot of sway with the board. He could rat me out. I went out of the community and was caught on camera. Going by their history, if the board found out, they'd probably kill Liona and me. "How do I know I can trust you?" I ask.

Winston sighs and takes a seat on one of his gray uncomfortable-looking chairs. He crosses his legs and adjusts his nighttime robe. "I would say that I've tried to help you before, so I'm probably someone you can trust, but honestly, I don't know. It seems like you're the one who wants something."

He's got a point. Plus, if he doesn't help, I could just kill him.

"Okay."

I reveal everything I just found out from Liona, starting with Lawrence being a major prick and ending with Lawrence being a major *evil* prick.

"Shit," Winston says once I'm finished. "So, you plan to ignore Liona's wishes, find a better disguise, and kill Lawrence?"

I shrug. "Something like that, I guess."

Winston sighs and stands up. "Well, you came to the right place. I have exactly what you need."

"Really? Thanks, man."

"I do think the plan to kill Lawrence needs some work-shopping. Actually, I think I have just the idea to solve all of this. But first, let's make you look less like an ogre. Follow me in here," Winston calls back, leading me to a room off the side.

I do as I'm told and enter what looks like a scientist's lab. There are vials of different color liquids in glass cabinets and chrome tools on steel tables.

"What is this place?" I ask while I gawk at my surroundings.

"It's my workroom. This is where I develop my newest potions and practice experiments."

"Is this what the other wizards' houses look like?" Although I had some ideas of what I thought Winston's home would look like, when I think about it, I'd never actually been into another wizard's house. I haven't been in almost any of the other magical creatures' houses when I think about it.

Winston laughs and pulls on a white lab coat from a hanger next to him. "No. The other wizards in this community are stuck in the past. I enjoy their slow way of living, but I make sure to travel as much as possible to stay up to date on all the new magical findings."

That makes sense. I can't imagine Old Man Willy, with his beard almost touching the floor, putting on a lab coat over his ancient and heavy robes.

Winston heads to the glass cabinet, bends over, and squints while pushing his glasses up the bridge of his nose. "Here it is," he says as he pulls out a vial with a dark purple liquid inside.

"What is that?" I walk closer to him, eyeing the vial in his hand.

Winston looks up, a goofy smile plastered on his face. "It's a potion that will make you human."

"Have you tested this before?" I take the vial from Winston, examining the strange glowing liquid.

His eyes dart, and he pulls at the collar of his coat. "Well... Not exactly."

"What does that mean?"

"It means no. I've never tried it. I'm hoping you'd be the guinea pig."

"Ah, fuck." I don't have a lot of options, but it would be pretty pathetic if I died before I even started trying to save Liona.

"I'm 99.999% that it works perfectly." He smiles. "It's not supposed to last forever, so if you hate it, you'll change back... at some point."

I hesitate for a second. "Okay, fine." I unscrew the lid. "But if I grow a tail or something, I'm beating the shit out of you."

"Don't worry, man. I'll come to LA with you to make sure it doesn't wear off too soon or fix it if something goes wrong."

"Come to LA with me?" I don't know if I want Winston tagging along and crashing my big romantic moment with Liona when we reunite. My cock hardens just thinking about it. "That's okay."

"I told you I have another plan to get Lawrence to drop the blackmail and the marriage. You're going to need me there for it to work. I don't know if you realize, but I also have some stake in this. I don't want the magical community to get discovered either."

I sigh. "Fine, but just be prepared that I'll be ripping Liona's clothes off the moment I see her." I hold the potion to my lips, knowing that if I don't take it now, I'll talk myself out of it.

"Oh, I won't mind that at all," he says devilishly.

I glare at him before bringing the bottle to my lips and chugging its contents in one gulp.

I wait for a second. "Well, now what?"

"I'm not sure how long it will take to work, but it should...."

A pain jolts through my stomach. "Fuck!" I yell and double over. I'm dizzy, and I drop to the floor, my vision tunneling.

The last thing I see before everything goes black is Winston peering over me. "Well, I'll be damned. I didn't expect that."

CHAPTER SIX

Liona

The last few days have been a waiting game. I'm waiting for Lawrence's lawyer to send over the prenup. Waiting to hear where and when the private ceremony will take place. Waiting for this horrible part of my life to be over. On the plus side, I've gotten to catch up on the movies that were released while I was gone. We have cable in the swamp, but cable and hotel movies are in a different tax bracket.

Lawrence has been funding my stay here at the Beverly Place Hotel, and I'm sure as hell making sure to rack up his room service bill. Filet mignon every night.

I do feel better now that I told Beck what's going on. I felt like such a bitch while eating caviar and knowing Beck was stuck at home thinking I was second-guessing our relationship. I should have just told him from the beginning. Getting him to let me leave when we were face to face would have been harder, but I should always be honest with him. I'll make it up to him later. I've also been renting premium adult movies on the hotel movie selection. I've got a list of things to try out on Beck when I get back to him.

My core heats. Maybe I should call Beck and we can have fun like we did last night. I'd never thought we'd experience phone sex, being rural swamp dwellers and all. I'd much rather have actual sex with my hunk of an ogre, but it did feel so naughty to make each other come from so many miles away.

As if hearing my horny thoughts, the hotel phone rings next to me from my nightside table. I pick myself up from my lounging position in the middle of the king-size bed and crawl to the phone, doing my best not to let the white robe fall off my body. I've just taken the most luxurious bath and my wet hair is wrapped in a fluffy white towel. I really shouldn't be enjoying this trip, but hey, I'm making the best out of a shitty situation.

"Hello?" I say in my most sultry voice.

"Are you in your room?" Beck's voice is determined.

"Uh, yes. Why?"

"Good." He hangs up.

My heart hammers in my chest and my mind races. *What the fuck?*

Someone knocks on my door aggressively.

"No," I say, frozen in place. That better not be Beck. That better be some singing telegram or some shit and not my seven-foot-tall ogre in some shitty disguise when I specifically told him not to come here.

Whomever it is knocks again.

I already know who it is, though—that arrogant knock.

I stomp to the door, fuming. I swing the door open, ready to yell at Beck for being so careless, but also ready to fuck the shit out of him because, come on, I'm only human.

"What..." I stop myself.

It's not Beck, but there is some resemblance. His eyes...

"Who the fuck are you?"

CHAPTER SEVEN

Liona

"Liona," he groans and charges for me, heat in his eyes.

Without even thinking, my fight-or-flight instincts take in. I slam the door on his smug and unusually handsome face, but before it clicks shut, he reaches out his hand and keeps it open.

"No way, fuck face!" I fight against him, trying with all my might to pull the door closed, but I'm no match. Within seconds, I'm on the floor, crawling away from the incredibly tall and robust stranger who stomps into my room, devouring me with his stare. I look around for things to throw at him, unfortunately only finding decorative pillows. I chuck them at his head, and he doesn't even attempt to stop them.

"Liona, it's me."

I freeze. "Beck?" I'm still petrified. His voice sounds like Beck, but he definitely isn't him. He's a human.

"Did you really think I'd let you go so easily? I'd follow you to the ends of the Earth. I'd watch the world burn for you," he says, his gaze intense, still stalking towards me. He's wearing tan linen shorts and a white button-down shirt with only the last two buttons fastened, revealing his broad and muscular chest. These are Beck's clothes.

"Hey, Liona." Winston walks in through the open doorway and closes it behind him.

"Winston? What's going on?" Seeing a familiar face eases my nerves, and I pick myself off the ground, finally aware that my measly bathrobe has probably revealed a nip slip one or two times in my attempt to get away. I fasten the belt tighter around my waist.

The tall stranger fixes his eyes down my body, licking his lips.

"We're here to rescue you!" Winston says. He's sporting a giddy grin and wears a light grey suit.

I examine the man before me, walking around him. "Beck, is that really you?"

"Yes." He gives a sheepish grin.

My chest constricts, and tears form at the corner of my eyes. Of course, he would come for me. Of course, he would find a way to save me. "Oh, Beck!" I exclaim, wrapping my arms around him and burying my face in his chest. He smells the same: sandalwood and earth.

He wraps his arms around my bottom and picks me up, bringing me to his eye level.

Even as a human, I think he's still seven feet tall. We're sure as hell not going to avoid any attention.

He gazes into my eyes and pushes a strand of my still-wet hair out of my face. "I missed you so much."

I cup his face and examine him. I don't know how I didn't realize it before, but he has some of the same features: a strong chiseled jaw, a head full of hair, and hazel eyes piercing my soul. But now his skin is a shade darker than mine, and his face has traces of stubble. He'll probably need to shave soon, or he'll have a beard. I don't hate the idea of having his stubble rub against all my sensitive spots.

"What did you do?" I question, still in disbelief, that my ogre is now a human man.

"Winston had a potion that turned me into a human. I wanted to help, but you said I couldn't come as an ogre."

I slap his chest. "I told you not to come at all."

He laughs. "But aren't you so glad I disobeyed?" He gives my ass a sensual squeeze, and my core immediately heats.

I grin, but my smile quickly melts.

"What's wrong?" His brow creases.

"Will you stay like this forever?" I caress his cheek. I'm not sure what magic made his transformation, and I don't want to admit it in case there's no way back, but I miss the ogre. I miss the green, the fangs, the monster that scares and thrills me at the same time.

Winston clears his throat. "Don't worry, Liona. I'm not sure how long the potion will last but it's temporary. That's why I'm here. To assist if it wears off too early. That and other reasons." He gives me a devilish smirk.

I'm unsure what he's implying, but I don't give it much thought and bring my attention back to Beck, who's searching my face as if to read my thoughts. "Do you like me better this way?"

I giggle. "I mean, you are hot, like we might not be able to get very far because every woman that looks at you will be begging to suck your dick, but no. I already miss my ogre." I kiss his full pink lips. "But it might be fun to explore a different man a few times." I run my hands down his chest.

He smacks my ass while I'm still in his arms and grits his teeth. "Naughty girl." He walks me back to the bed. "And who said anything about just a *few* times? I've got big plans for you." He throws me on the bed and covers me with his body.

I'm ready to go and see what his human dick can do, but an urgent dread presses my mind. I pull back from our embrace. "Don't we have things to discuss? You know, I'm being blackmailed to get married to an incestual supervillain? Shouldn't we figure out a plan to get out of this?" I'd thought there was no way to get out of this forced marriage that didn't end up hurting the people I loved, but now seeing Beck in his human form, I think anything is possible.

Beck rolls his eyes and lowers his mouth to my ear. "I can't think clearly until I fuck you."

I moan softly, then my attention snaps towards the door, remembering we're not alone.

Winston is seated at the small chair and table in the corner, his blazer resting on the table, and his white sleeves are rolled up, revealing his muscular and veiny forearms. He's gripping the armrests as he watches us intently.

I gulp, trying to gather the right words. I never thought I wanted someone to watch me, but seeing the hunger in Winston's eyes makes me second-guess my feelings. The thoughts of him staring at us like that while I'm being pleasured — my core heats even more.

Beck notices my gaze and snaps his attention to Winston. "Winston, get the fuck out of here." He looks back towards me, raises up to his knees, and works on untying my robe. "Hurry," he barks again.

I keep my gaze on Winston. He winks at me before standing up and swinging his blazer over his shoulder. "Alright, I can see I'm not wanted at the moment. I'll see the front desk about getting my own room." He stops and looks at me before shutting the door. "Hopefully, one right next door."

I breathe out, the room immediately becoming less thick without his presence.

"Finally," Beck groans and rips my robe open, revealing my breasts, my nipples already hard from so much anticipation. "Ah, fuck. You're so fucking perfect." He leans down, captures my mouth, and trails down my body until he reaches my nipples. He laps at them with his human tongue, alternating from one side to the other.

I must admit, it feels odd not to have the slight prick of his fangs. I miss the sensation. But I'm so aroused right now, and I know it will take everything in me not to explode when he touches my pussy.

As if reading my thoughts, he brings his hand down to my core, spreading my lips and running his finger up and down. "Oh, my god, you're so wet," he moans against my breast; his breath is hot against my skin.

I gasp for words. "I'm ready for you."

"I need a taste first." He crawls down my body, lapping me up like he's dying of thirst. "You taste so good."

I feel his scruff rub against me, and the pain mixed with pleasure is intoxicating. "I don't know how long I can last," I cry, tugging at his hair, still shoulder length but now much silkier. I want to savor this moment with him as a new man. I almost feel like I'm cheating on Beck, even though I know it's him. It feels so naughty, and I love it.

He continues to lap me up, bringing me so close to the edge that I almost can't take it anymore. I pull at his hair harder, wanting him inside me as I come. If anything, this makes him more determined. He focuses on my clit, applying the perfect amount of pressure with the slightest movement.

"Fuck," I yell as my orgasm rushes through me. My body convulses, and I cry out in pure ecstasy. I push into his tongue, finally accepting my defeat and milking my first orgasm in what feels so long (a day).

Beck doesn't stop until my body stills.

"I wanted to come with you inside of me," I groan.

Beck crawls over me. "You don't think I can make you come more than once? Do you really think this human form could limit my abilities to pleasure you?" He nuzzles into my neck. "No, my little pet. I could make you come as many times as I see fit. In fact, I might not let you sleep tonight. Just bounce you on my dick until you've soaked the whole bed with your sweet juices." He nips at me, and the orgasm that just passed seems like it happened centuries ago. I'm ready to be bouncing on that dick.

"Lay on your back. I want to see all of you. It's not every day I get to be fucked by a stranger."

I expect Beck to push back because he always loves to show me some resistance to orders, but he does as I say and lays beside me, reaching for me to climb on top of him the second his back hits the bed.

He's so big I feel like a tiny parasitic insect with my legs wrapped around his middle. I unbutton his last two remaining buttons and run my hands up his chest, rippling with bolder-like muscles. "Your skin is so soft," I say in a small voice.

"I know. I hate it. Only you can be soft."

I squint at him. "I must say, I do miss rubbing myself along your rough and muscley chest, but this is nice too. I could touch you all day."

"Well, in that case, I might just keep my skin this way."

"No." I lean over and capture his lips in mine, running my hands along his rough chin. "But it did feel nice for your face to be so rough when you were eating me out."

"Oh, yeah?" He smiles at me and picks me up, placing my backside against his rock-hard cock.

I moan. "Oh, so forward. Is there something that you want from me?"

He grinds against my ass. "Inside you. Now." He rolls his head back and moans.

"Patience, my big strong man." I crawl down him and work on ripping off his pants. His cock springs out, hard and dripping. "It's the same size!" I squeal in delight. My mouth waters, and I lean over, wrapping my lips around his head. He tastes so salty and sweet. I slide up and down on his thigh, coating him with my liquid. I roll my lips to the base of him, gagging while water spills from my eyes.

His hips jolt into me, going deeper than he's ever before.

I come up. "Jesus, you can't do that without warning. You're too big for that."

He grabs my arm in a flash, dragging me up to him. "No more playing around. I need your cunt stretched around me."

Both of us fumble as we position his cock at my entrance. He gives shallow thrusts until his entire length is inside of me. I'm so wet that it's easy for him to slide in, even with his size. When he finally hits my wall, he rams into me, losing himself.

I pick myself up until I'm riding on him upwards, my tits jiggling with each of his thrusts.

He grabs me, pulling me back to blanket him and kiss me. With each thrust, I grow closer and closer to my edge until my body turns to mush, and every one of my nerves is on fire. We both yell in unison, and our orgasms crash through us like a tidal wave.

Our bodies still, but I cling onto him, nuzzling my head into his neck. I breathe in his sweet sweat. I've missed this too much.

I break our unison of labored breaths. "Let's make a pact. We'll never go without sex for that long again," I demand.

Beck laughs. "I don't know. That was fucking fantastic. Maybe we should limit ourselves more often."

I pop up and smack his chest. "Don't say such a thing."

He chuckles and grabs me, swinging me down on the bed and straddling me. "Don't start already. I could go for round two if you tempt me." He loves me for my naughtiest of behaviors. I can already feel him hardening.

I laugh. "See? It hasn't even been ten seconds, and you're ready to fuck again. You really think we could last a few days?"

"No," he says before crashing down into another kiss.

We roll around in the sheets for a few more minutes, grabbing and feeling each other, teasing each other until we almost really start again, but I break away. "Alright, I think we really should talk about what we're going to do to get out of this mess."

Beck sighs and rolls on his back. He stares up at the ceiling and taps his fingers against his chest.

I prop my head up with my hand and watch him, ready for him to reveal his big plan.

He takes in a big breath of air with his pointer finger extended as if he just got the best idea. "You know what?"

He turns to me, and I lean in. "What?"

"Let's just figure this out in the morning." He springs like a wildcat and pulls himself on top of me, kissing me down my neck.

I giggle but don't resist. Well, don't resist *much*. I always must play a little bit of a game. I guess we're going for round two. And honestly, probably rounds three and four.

CHAPTER EIGHT

Beck

I sip my coffee, keeping my eyes glued to all the people passing by. "Are you sure nothing is wearing off? People are staring at me," I whisper to Liona.

I've only been a human for twenty-four hours, and I'm already hating it. It feels so odd to be doing everyday things, such as eating "brunch" at a busy restaurant in the center of LA. We're sitting outside on the porch, but it doesn't make me feel any less crowded. The servers, the people next to us, passersby on the street, it's all too much. Humans need another plague or something.

She looks at Winston, sitting across the table from us, and they both chuckle. She turns to me and tucks a strand of hair behind my ear. "Beck, you're a seven-foot-tall Greek god. People are going to stare. Probably every woman, and man for that matter, want to fuck you." She takes a sip of her tea.

"I guess now I know what it feels like to be you." I munch on a piece of my toast. "I hate it. This is why I live in a swamp. I don't like the attention."

Liona leans over me. "You seemed to like the attention I gave you last night." She kisses me. "And this morning."

I lean to her ear. "I only like attention from you. That's why I keep you prisoner, with me so that you can be my sex slave in solitude."

She slaps my arm.

"You're not very good at whispering," Winston says, giving us a bemused grin.

Liona's cheeks blush, and she clears her throat. "So, Winston, Beck said that you have a plan to get Lawrence to drop the blackmail and get me out of marrying that prick.

A plan that doesn't involve murder." She takes a bite of her pancakes. "Although I wouldn't mind seeing Lawrence die, it's too messy."

"You and I agree on that point."

"I rather kill him," I grunt, scarfing down more of my food.

Liona watches me for a second and then laughs. I realize I'm probably eating more like a monster and less like a human, but Liona doesn't bother to correct me. She just shakes her head and brushes a strand of chocolate brown hair behind her ear. Every angle of Liona is perfect, even her profile. I can't take my eyes off the gentle swoop of her nose, full eyelashes, and pouty lips, but Winston clears his throat, bringing my attention back to the issue.

"I do have a plan, one that I think will solve all of our problems and even check off a place I've been meaning to visit."

"Go on," I bark. Winston is theatrical and will want to drag this out if he can. I don't have the patience to wait.

The sooner I get this over with and have Liona back in my swamp to myself, the better.

"There's a potion."

"Another potion?" Liona questions.

"Yes, this one is called a 'Charming Potion'."

"What does it do?" She leans closer to Winston. Her breasts spill out at the top of her brown tank top, and I can't help but notice Winston lose his attention for a second. My grip tightens around my fork.

He continues, "It makes the person who consumes it utterly charming and compliant. We just have to slip it into Lawrence's drink, and he'll do whatever we say. We can get him to destroy all the evidence of Beck's past LA visit and the whereabouts of the community."

"Why didn't you mention this sooner?" I ask angrily. "Do you have it with you?"

"No. This isn't a potion I made, but I'm flattered you would think I have such power. There is someone in town, though, that has it."

"Well, who is it?" I ask.

"Her name is G.M. Fairy."

"G.M. Fairy?" Liona questions.

"Yes, it's short for Fairy Godmother. She owns a club called 'Happy Ever Endings.' It's a private club reserved for magical beings. Well, magical beings that can make it there without being spotted. We can go tonight."

"How do you know about this club?" I ask. In all my years as a magical being, I've never heard of a magical club. I guess it wouldn't matter anyways since I've always been unable to leave the swamp.

Winston smiles. "There are many perks for being able to pass as a normal human. I make sure to travel often. Clubs like these are my favorite reason for traveling, and it's part of why I wanted to come to LA with you. Happy Ever Endings is one of my favorite places."

I give him a skeptical look. Winston's a weird guy, but I guess he's our best bet in figuring this all out.

"Do you think she'll give it to us?" Liona asks, bringing the conversation back on track.

I run my hands through my hair, still not used to its soft feeling. "If she doesn't, we'll make her give it to us."

Winston takes a sip of his tea, places it on its saucer, and waves his hands in refusal. "No need for that. G.M. Fairy is a businesswoman. She'll be happy to give us the potion. As long as we give her something in return."

Liona looks at me and then back to Winston. "What kind of payment?"

Winston winks at her. "Nothing you won't be more than willing to give."

I slam a fist on the table. "What the fuck does that mean?"

"Calm down," Winston soothes. "I'm not sure entirely, but she's a reasonable woman, and she won't make you do anything you're uncomfortable with. Let's just head there tonight and see what she says."

I relax a bit, rolling my shoulders back. "Fine, but if she's difficult, we're doing this my way."

Liona ignores my remark, her eyes aglow with excitement. "What should I wear?"

I can't imagine why she seems so giddy to go to a night-club. There are already too many people here at this cafe. I know what nightclubs are like, crowded rooms stuffed with sweaty bodies. Disgusting. But maybe Liona misses people. Sure, she stays social in the village back home, but perhaps she misses going out and getting dressed up. I'll be a good sport. I know we're on a mission, but I'll make sure she has a good time.

"The less you wear, the better," Winston whispers.

I grunt at Winston and then put my arm around her shoulder. I do enjoy seeing Liona in as little clothes as possible, but I don't know if I want everyone else to see her that way.

"Come on, Beck. You have a beautiful woman on your arm. Do you really think she would leave you for anyone else? Let her flaunt what she's got a little bit. You might find that you like it."

Liona looks up at me with a flirty smirk.

I kiss her lips. "Alright, if you want to wear practically nothing, I won't get in your way. As long as I'm the only one laying a finger on you." I kiss down her neck.

She gives a shuddering breath.

Winston claps his hands together. "Well, this is going to be fun!"

CHAPTER NINE

Liona

"This is it?" I look up in astonishment at the unlit warehouse on the city's outskirts. I pull down my skin-tight black dress, suddenly feeling overdressed.

Beck and I had spent the day going in and out of shops near my hotel. Beck hated every second of it, but I made it up to him by pulling him into one of the dressing rooms and sucking his dick. I think Beck *loves* shopping now.

I finally decided on a cotton black halter dress with cut-outs on the side. My tits look fantastic, and Beck can't keep his hands off my ass, so I imagine it looks great back there too. I just wish my new favorite outfit wasn't making its debut at a place where crackheads probably pick up their fix.

Winston laughs and adjusts his collar. "I told you it was a secret club. They have to make it look inconspicuous." He's wearing a tight-fitting white button-down, his sleeves rolled up, and his curly brown hair is gelled back. I'd never admit it out loud, but he looks sexy as hell. He doesn't even hold a candle to Beck, though, wearing a black button-down, also rolled up to reveal his muscular and veiny forearms. We purchased this and his black slacks while getting my dress. His shoulder-length hair is still unruly, but his facial hair is shaved down tight. God, I want to rip off all his clothes. I bite my lip thinking about how he'd look in this outfit as an ogre.

Winston heads towards the door of the building, lit only by a single flickering light directly overhead.

Beck puts his arm around me as if he's unsure about this location as I am. "You sure about this?" he asks in a low tone.

Winston grins back at us. "I promise. You're going to love this place." He makes a series of distinct raps on the black door. Nothing happens.

I speak up. "Are you sure..."

Suddenly, a rectangular compartment on the door slides open, revealing dark grey eyes. "Password?" asks a low voice.

"All good things happen after dark," Winston whispers back.

The compartment slides shut, and the door swings open a moment later. Winston leads the way inside, and the door slams closed behind us. We're in a small coat room. The grey eyes belong to a massive man with a hoop nose ring. He's a foot taller than Beck. I know this is a magical club, so I study him, looking for signs of mysticism. Sure enough, tiny horns barely poke out from his mop of curly hair. The man doesn't say anything to us. He opens the door across from us, holding his arm for us to pass through.

The moment the door opens, music thumps out. It's not blaring or fast paced, but it almost sounds like the rhythm of a heartbeat. It takes a second for my eyes to adjust. It's dark but neon purple handrails run along the sides of a narrow pathway.

"Here we are!" Winston looks back at us as he walks forward.

Walking further down the long hallway, I notice the walls have pictures of different couples fucking each other. I stop to stare at a picture of a busty woman being eaten out by a muscular guy. Upon closer inspection, I realize the woman has wings, and the man has a dragon tail. It's then I pay closer attention to the sounds. Soft moans come from all around us. My core heats. "Winston, what kind of club is this?"

He stops and turns to me. "I told you, it's a magical club."

"But what type of magical club?"

Beck swivels his head around at the walls as if my questions finally make him hear the moans and notice the explicit pictures.

"It's a sex club. Wasn't that obvious?" He looks at us, dumbfounded.

"I mean, now it is!" I instinctually pull my dress down, suddenly feeling self-conscious even if a rush of adrenaline floods through me.

"Winston," Beck growls and pulls me closer. "Why didn't you tell us you were taking us to a sex club?"

Winston sighs. "It's called Happily Ever Endings. I thought that was obvious enough." He runs his hands through his slick hair. "Just follow me. All we have to do is meet with G.M. Fairy. I didn't realize you two would be such a pair of buzzkills."

I gulp and catch up to him. "We're not going to be buzzkills, and I can't say I'm not curious. I just wish you would have told us before we were here."

"You're curious?" Beck asks from beside me.

My cheeks heat and I look up at him. "I mean, yeah, a little. I can't say the thought doesn't get me hot and bothered."

Beck's eyes darken as he looks down at me. I can't thoroughly read his expression in the dark, but it seems like my words lit a fire in him. He's got that hungry look about him that I love so much.

We continue down the hallway until we're in a lobby. Two identical women with matching black bobs and latex jumpsuits sit at a desk before us.

Winston walks up to them and leans against the black marble counter. "Winston the Wizard, party of three."

I push myself against the counter, wanting to see what magical quality they possess. They look normal, but as I peer closer, I realize their skin sparkles more than sparkly body mist.

One of the women types something on her computer while the other continues to flip through documents. "Here you are." She places a black card on the counter that reads "Happily Ever Endings" in big gold lettering.

"This will get you into the door for the main playroom. All the other rooms are located off the side of this room. The waiver you signed mentioned all the rules. Did you all read those?"

"Yes," Winston replies before I even have a chance to look confused. He grabs the keys and asks, "We're supposed to have an appointment with G.M. Fairy. Where should I meet her?"

The other woman clicks a few buttons on her computer. "She's just finishing up a meeting now. One of us will come find you when she's ready."

"Great. Thanks." Winston turns back to us.

"Enjoy yourself," one of the women calls as Winston leads us to a set of doors to our left.

Once we're far enough away, I whisper to Winston, "What are the rules?"

Winston waves his hand and speaks loud enough for both of us to hear. "Just normal stuff. Don't touch people that don't want you to touch them. Don't be a dick." He slides the key through the reader, and the big metal door opens. "After you."

The music and moans blare even louder. I glance up at Beck, who's already looking down at me. I nod, take a deep breath and step inside.

I gasp once I see the scene before me. In the middle of a large room is a circular elevated stage amidst red velvet lounge chairs littered with people watching, making out, performing oral sex, or just straight-up fucking. On the stage is a mermaid tied to a table, her breasts exposed. Another woman with a horse tail and hoofs, wearing a latex suit, walks around her, a whip in her hand. I can't help but stare.

"Oh, before I forget." Winston stands in front of me and pulls something out of his pocket. "These will help make this place more enjoyable."

I glance down at the sugary orbs that look like glowing candy. "What is that? Ecstasy?"

Winston chuckles. "It's kind of like that but without all the bad effects and horrible comedowns. They're called

Gumdrop Buttons. They're magical pills allowing you to orgasm five or six times. It's one of my inventions."

I look up at Beck. He just shrugs, takes one from Winston, and pops it into his mouth.

Okay, so Beck is down for this.

I grab one from Winston and do the same.

Winston smiles. "There we go! I knew you two would be fun." He walks toward the nearest velvet seat but turns back to us. "I'm going to enjoy the show, but you two should explore some other rooms before meeting with Ms. Fairy. I've been here a handful of times, so I've already seen everything."

I turn to Beck once Winston's out of earshot. "Are you ready to explore?" I run my hands up his chest.

He sucks in a sharp breath. "Is that what you want to do?"

I lean closer. "As long as I'm with you, I'm down for anything." My nipples harden. I'm not sure if it's whatever Winston gave me already having its effect or if it's just everything around me. The noise from the people around us, the pair performing on the stage, the way Beck looks right now, all of it's enough to accelerate me toward that edge.

"Let's have some fun," Beck says as he leads me toward the edge of the large room.

CHAPTER TEN

Beck

Liona and I walk hand in hand down a hallway with doors on either side. We've opened a few to find different bedrooms, some with interesting equipment, such as crosses, leather couches, and whips and chains. We haven't decided to start anywhere, although my heart is racing, and it's taking everything in me not to pull Liona into one of them and get this first fuck out.

I would think that Winston dropping this sex-club surprise would make me furious. I'm usually so possessive of Liona, and the thoughts of other men walking by, watching her, and wanting to fuck her should make my blood boil, but I don't feel that way. In fact, I have this urge to take her where everyone can see. I want everyone to know she is mine and just how good I can make her feel.

We approach the end of the long hallway that opens into a circular area with windows on the walls. There are velvet couches situated in front of these windows. The room is dimly lit, but brighter light illuminates from the windows. As we walk closer, I realize the windows allow onlookers to view people fucking in private rooms. There are only three rooms currently in use. One has a single woman using a long dildo by herself. One has three people, two women and one man, all Faye. They're all three intertwined on a large bed-like sofa that faces the window. The last one contains a man who looks entirely made of wood. Although we can't hear anything from inside the rooms, I see his mouth move, and his nose extends longer and longer. He lays down on a couch, and a woman sits on his face, impaling herself with his larger-than-life wooden nose.

As Liona and I walk around the room, we can't hear anything from them. The only sounds are the soft music from the speakers and the onlookers on the couches who are either pleasuring themselves or pleasuring each other.

Liona stops in front of the window of the first woman.

I take a step back, wanting to see her reaction.

The woman sits on a black leather couch. She has never ending golden blond hair, which trails all around the room, and her tits are large and perky. She's not wearing a stitch of clothing except for black high heels. One of her hands circles her clit while the other drives a toy deep inside her. The woman's face is flushed, and her eyes are drowsy slits. She opens her eyes in surprise as if noticing Liona in front of her. The woman gets to her knees and crawls closer to the glass, pressing her breasts against it without stopping pleasuring herself.

Liona slowly walks closer to the glass as if magnified by what she's seeing. When her hands are pressed atop the woman behind the glass, she looks back at me as if asking me for permission.

I nod and take a seat on the chair closest to me. God, do I want to see more.

She drops to her knees and presses herself against the glass, meeting her lips to the woman.

The woman returns the gesture, making out with Liona, with only the glass separating them.

Liona's hand trails down her body, lingering at the hem of her dress, and she grazes it, testing if she should really dive into herself.

I want to tell her to do it, to touch herself, but I don't want to interrupt.

The woman's movements speed up as if she's reaching her climax. Liona licks the glass, and the woman does the same, their tongues a matching frenzy of soft pink.

It's then I notice all the onlookers. Men and women have formed a crowd around Liona and the woman in the glass.

Liona's breath heavies, and she rubs herself against the glass until the woman reaches her edge and sputters into frantic movements from ecstasy. Liona looks back at me, fire in her eyes, and stands up and walks toward me.

She places her hands on the armrests of my chair and leans forward so her mouth is against my ear. "I want you to fuck me in one of these rooms, and I want everyone to watch."

I can't suppress my groan at her words. I pull her closer to me and capture her mouth. "Yes, please." I nip at her lip.

She grabs my hand and leads me to one of the empty rooms, opening the door on the left of the window. A screen to the side indicates that the room is clean and ready to use. When we're both inside, I lock the door behind us.

The room matches the others. There's a black leather couch, and low purple lights line the floor in the corners.

Liona watches me as she walks backward to the couch.

I stalk closer. "Are you sure you want to do this?" I can already glimpse a crowd forming outside and sitting on the velvet couches and chairs surrounding our window.

"Let's just play a little." She removes the space between us, running her hands up my chest.

I suck in a breath of air. Her touch has always felt electric, but something about being here, people watching us, and probably whatever Winston gave us makes me feel like my blood is dynamite. I grab the back of her head, pulling her into me as I capture her lips. I grab her ass in one swift movement, and she wraps her legs around my torso. I walk her back to the couch and sit her in the middle.

When I pull away, she gasps for air. "Come back."

I don't pull away from her stare as I drop to my knees and run my hands up her thighs.

She moans and clutches her breasts.

I slowly pull her dress higher and higher up her thighs, letting my touch trail in its wake. "Let them see those perfect tits." I look up at her as she slowly shimmies her shoulders, letting the straps of her dress drop.

Although we can't hear anything besides the low music in this room, I can feel the energy shift from outside. I turn back to watch as onlookers gawk at us. Some are pleasuring themselves, their eyes wide open, not wanting to miss a thing. Some have partners bouncing up and down on their laps, fucking each other as they imagine my perfect Liona.

"Do you see them out there?" I whisper to her as I tease her with licks just outside her core. "They all wish they were fucking you. Do you want to show them what it looks like to have you lost in yourself?"

"Yes," she cries.

I push her dress up more, revealing her perfect pussy. "You didn't wear any underwear. You naughty girl." I run my finger through her curls.

"Maybe you should punish me."

"Not right now. Right now, I want to make you feel so good." I drag my tongue against her opening, shuttering once I taste her sweetness.

Her body bucks against me. The anticipation seeps out of her, begging to release.

But I have a show to put on. I need to take my time.

Liona runs her hands through my hair; small sounds escape her lips.

I lap up her liquids, moving my tongue slowly, front to back. When I reach her core, I poke in my tongue, imagining my cock penetrating her.

"Beck, I don't know how long I'll last," she whimpers.

"Come whenever you're ready, baby. We've got plenty of rooms to explore."

I pull back and dip my finger inside of her, giving the audience room to see how gushing wet she is from me. I fuck her with my fingers until I hear her breaths quicken. I bring my mouth to her clit, flicking it with my tongue as I drive my fingers deep inside her.

She sits up, grabbing my head as her orgasm washes over her. Her tits bounce on my head, and she writhes her body against me until every last ounce of pleasure releases from her.

When she finally stills, she falls to her back, catching her breath.

A soft knock comes from the window.

Winston stares at us from across the glass, a smirk on his lips. He motions for us to exit. It must

be time to meet with G.M. Fairy, and I can't help but wonder if she got a peek of our performance as well.

CHAPTER ELEVEN

Liona

I should be embarrassed. Weeks ago, if I had known I'd let a crowd full of people watch me get eaten out and have an earth-shattering orgasm, I probably would have laughed my ass off. Sure, the thought would have thrilled me, but to think I would actually do it would seem outrageous. But now here I am, still vibrating from the pleasure that ran through me. In fact, I want a whole lot more to run through me, starting with Beck, and I want the entire world to see. What is wrong with me? What beast has been unleashed?

I slowly pull down my dress and adjust my straps, watching as the crowd's mouth waters at my smallest movement. Goddammit, this kind of power could get addicting. I follow Beck out of the room. Winston is waiting for us, and by the look on his face, he saw everything. My cheeks heat and a warm feeling rushes through me.

"Bravo!" he exclaims. "Best show of the night so far." He pats Beck on the back and gives me a devilish grin.

Beck looks slightly annoyed but doesn't remark.

"Beck, Liona, I'd like you to meet the lady of the hour, G.M. Fairy." He motions to a woman seated at one of the red velvet armchairs in front of our window. She rises to her feet and then flutters a few inches off the ground, gliding towards us. She has an unearthly glow to her, and her lavender dress seems to be lit by starlight. She's an older woman but her face is smooth and her eyes sparkle with a youthful glow. She doesn't look like someone who owns an underground sex club. More like a woman who grants wishes and turns pumpkins into horse-drawn carriages.

"It's a pleasure to meet you both. It seems you two have natural talent." The gray-haired woman extends her hand towards me while adjusting her small glasses perched at the tip of her nose.

My cheeks warm as I grab her small hand. I can't believe I'm about to ask this woman a favor after she watched me in my most vulnerable moment. But hey, maybe that will work out in my favor.

"Winston was telling me I'd enjoy you two, but I must say." She looks Beck up and down as she reaches to shake his hand. "You're missing something."

"Nice to meet you. I'm actually an ogre, and Winston gave me a potion to make myself look like a human," Beck says as he shakes her hand.

The woman nods. "Ah, yes, that's it. I can tell you're lacking some color. Hopefully, he can return you to your original state before the night ends." She winks and then flies ahead of us. "Follow me, and let's chat in my office."

The three of us follow her to the end of a long hallway to a room guarded by two heavily built trolls in black sunglasses. How did I miss them before? One of the trolls opens the door for us, and the other stares us down as we follow G.M. Fairy inside.

The room is a large open space with a roaring fireplace, oriental carpets, sprawling bookcases, and glass jars and vials on every surface. A large floor-to-wall window faces a roaring ocean below a jagged cliff edge.

"How is that your view? We're not by an ocean," I ask, so awed by my surroundings that I completely lose my manners.

"It's a charm, darling. I can change it to any scene I want." She sits in the plush, purple armchair and snaps her fingers before crossing her legs. The scene suddenly changes to a volcano erupting with angry red lava. "Now, why don't you three have a seat and tell me what you desire." She motions to three smaller chairs that magically appear before her. "I must say, I'm not usually one for last-minute appointments, but Winston is a dear friend of mine, so you all are in luck." She gives Winston a wink, who returns her gesture.

I can't help but wonder *how* well they know each other.

"Thank you for having us, Ms. Fairy," I say as I sit.

"I can see you two are enjoying yourself, and I hope that whatever you wish, we can make it worth both of our whiles." She flicks her wrist, and a cup of piping hot tea appears in her hand. She blows on it before taking a sip.

I'm in awe. In just a few short minutes since I've known her, she's displayed her power repeatedly. I don't know if this is all a ruse for her to get us to do something for her, but whatever it is, it's working. I'm hoping that maybe she can help me out of this fucked marriage.

Beck clears his throat. "Winston says that you have a potion that could help us." He leans forward in his chair.

"Oh, did he? Well, I do usually have the answers to everyone's problems. Whether it's power, money, or sex, I've got the answer, but nothing is free. What is it you desire, and I'll name my price."

Winston speaks up. "They need the Charming Potion."

G.M. Fairy laughs. "Well, of course, you do. That's the most powerful potion I have yet, but also dangerous. What do you need it for? Surely an ogre such as yourself should be able to get people to do what you want, and if not that, I'm sure your little pet here would be able to influence them with her... *assets.*" She smirks and takes another sip of her tea.

Beck grips the armrests on his chair, and he furrows his brows.

I put my hand on my forearm and search for his eyes. His shoulders relax once our eyes meet.

I turn back to G.M. Fairy to address her. "We are trying to solve this problem without a mess. Discretion is of the utmost urgency. I'm being blackmailed into marrying a powerful and evil man, and we need the potion to eliminate the evidence." I straighten my shoulder. She may think I'm a stupid bimbo sex slave, but I want her to know I mean business. "Now, tell us your price for this potion so we can carry the fuck on with our plan."

G.M. Fairy snaps, and her tea disappears. She uncrosses and crosses her legs, her face changing to a bemused smirk. "Well, well, well, it seems as if this pet has some spunk. I like that." She gets up from her chair and floats around us. "Luckily, you've got me on a good day, so my price is more than reasonable. I'd like you two to perform tonight. Of course, I'd want you back in your ogre form. This is a magical sex club, after all."

"Perform?" Beck growls.

"Why, it wouldn't be much different than what I witnessed you two doing. Except this time, it would be on a larger stage with a longer set time, you know, higher production value."

My cheeks heat. The thought of being on that mainstage, being fucked for so many eyes to see, genuinely thrills me, but I don't know how Beck feels about it, especially after G.M. Fairy insulted his strength and referred to me as his pet.

He speaks up. "That's it? You just want us to fuck on your stage, and you'll give us the potion?"

G.M. Fairy laughs and then flutters to a bar cart, picks up a crystal decanter, and pours herself a small shot of the brown liquid. She takes a swig and speaks to us without turning. "For now. I'll have another favor to ask you in the future, a business proposition, but we don't need to worry about that now. You two seem to already have a lot on your plate."

Beck doesn't take his eyes off her. "How do I know this *business proposition* won't put us in more trouble than we started with?"

G.M. Fairy flutters back to us and leans against her chair. "I guess you'll just have to trust me. Winston and I have worked together several times, and I've always made sure that our deals were equally beneficial. Don't you agree, Winston?"

Winston speaks up, "Yes, definitely."

"Good, it's settled then. You two will perform in half an hour, I'll give you your potion, and you'll be on your way to happily ever after. Everyone's happy."

I look towards Beck, trying to gauge where he stands.

He just searches my face as if doing the same.

Although owing an unknown debt to G.M. Fairy seems like a risky deal, it seems like our only option. Besides, performing on that stage seems like my wet dreams come true. How horrible could her business proposition be if her first payment is me getting to fulfill all my sexual desires?

"Well," I say. "I guess we've got a show to put on."

Beck nods at my words and a fire lights behind his eyes.

Winston claps his hands together.

G.M. Fairy flutters to the door. "Great! Let's get a move on. We've got a show to prepare for, and you," she looks to Beck, "need to return to your ogre form.

CHAPTER TWELVE

Liona

G.M. Fairy said what we're already wearing works for the show. Although I enjoyed the leather out-fits I saw on the performers when we first arrived, I'd be the most comfortable in my clothes, even if they wouldn't be on for long. Beck has already taken his shirt off.

We got to choose our stage setup, and there were many options. Even though the bondage tables, the crosses, and the swings genuinely thrilled me, I wanted to go simpler for our first rodeo. We decided on an oversized chair that almost looks like a throne. Beck was the first to suggest it.

He wants my body to be the star of the show and to have me draped over him.

"Are you sure you want to do this?" Beck asks as he sits on the ornate red velvet chair. He leans back, rests his muscular arms on the armrest, and spreads his legs, allowing me to climb on his lap. A red curtain covers us from the view of the already gathering audience. It's just me and him for now.

I lean over him, resting my hands on his forearms and situating my breasts to his line of vision. "I think it's only fair that we share the pleasure we get from each other with others. It's too great for just us." I kiss his lips.

When I pull away, his eyes are still closed and he leans back, savoring the moment. He opens them and pulls me on his lap. "Are you sure you'll be okay fucking me as an ogre again?" He reaches into his pocket and pulls out the small green vial, the potion G.M. Fairy gave him to turn him back into an ogre. She states that this one won't have the same adverse effects as the human potion, so he won't pass out after taking it.

I twist my body and wrap my arms around his neck. "I want nothing more than to fuck an ogre before a crowd." I kiss him, pushing my tongue into his mouth, and rub my hands against his stubbly human face.

Beck pulls back, bites off the cork top off the vial and gulps the contents in one chug.

I watch as his face slowly contorts back to his ogre form. His skin changes to olive green, his hair becomes coarse, his muscles grow larger, and his fangs slide out from his lips. My core immediately heats. God, I've missed my ogre. I can barely help myself. I slip my hands into his shirt, feeling his rough skin as my lips meet his. This show better get a move on because I can't wait much longer.

"Hold your horses, you two." G.M. Fairy flutters into our curtained enclosure. "Remember, pace yourselves. People want an experience. Ah, it's nice to see you in your ogre form. So much better."

I pull away from our embrace. "Is there anything we should *do* in a certain order or anything?"

She flies over to me, adjusting the top of my dress so my breasts are almost spilling out. I slap her hands away, but she doesn't flinch.

"Nope, just do whatever you want. As long as the crowd can see and as long as it's not over in the first five minutes, we should be good. Alright, you two, break a leg." And with that, she zooms out as fast as she came.

I can't help but be surprised at how odd this whole thing is. G.M. Fairy talks like we're about to perform Westside Story. I guess that's how you talk when this is your everyday life. Can't say I'm not a little jealous.

I lie back against Beck, placing my arms over his.

"You ready?" he whispers in my ear.

The music changes and increases its volume. The curtain around us slowly starts to rise.

"I'm ready," I say through labored breaths, already feeling the weight of the anticipation.

Beck kisses my neck and I savor the delicious feel of his fangs rubbing against me.

I open my eyes and glance at the audience below us. I can barely see them from how dim the room is. The only light is the low circle of purple surrounding us. Every seat is taken; singles, couples, throuples, and more are arranged in various positions on the couches and chairs. I scan more as Beck's hand wanders to my breast, lightly circling my nipple. I spot G.M. Fairy in the front, her glasses resting on the tip of her nose. She's seated in a similar chair to ours, except it's purple and smaller. She looks as if she's observing an opera. It makes me nervous but also stirs something in me. I want to please her.

I notice a man a few seats down from her, his eyes intense as he grips the armrests of his chair. It's Winston. I'd known he'd seen Beck and me in the smaller room, but now I feel so much more vulnerable. There's no glass separating us, and my bits are front and center.

Beck must notice my heart rate increasing because he whispers in my ear, "How ya doing?"

I exhale, his gruff voice bringing me back to the moment.

"There's a lot of people here," I whisper.

"They're all here to see you." His other hand, not fondling my breast, trails down my body until it's at the hem of my dress. "And they want to see this pretty pussy of yours. Should we show them?" His fingers trace the inside of my leg.

"Yes," I gasp, letting my head fall back against his chest. My core throbs as if he hasn't touched me in ages.

He continues to caress me lightly, teasing the crowd and myself, as he runs his finger up and down my thigh, getting closer and closer to the part of me that aches for him.

I moan and wiggle, trying to direct him to my core.

Beck grabs my wrists and whispers, "I'm in control. You just relax and let me be the one to decide how you're pleasured."

His words cause more wetness to seep out of me. "God, I need you inside of me." I don't whisper. I want the audience to hear my words. I want them to know how much I want this.

Beck kisses up and down my neck, letting his tongue trail. Finally, he grabs the bottom of my dress and pulls it upwards, revealing all of me. "Spread those legs, baby. I want everyone to see how wet you are."

I push back and bring my feet onto the chair, spreading myself wide.

"Good girl." He lightly drags his finger up and down my folds. "Oh God, I can already tell you're gushing." He pushes his finger deeper but still caresses me softly. He brings his finger to his mouth and licks my liquids. "You taste so good."

My head lulls back and I cry out in desperation. "Please don't stop touching me."

He gives a gruff chuckle. "Look at you using your manners. Such a good girl." He dives two fingers into me, hard and fast, fucking me with his fingers.

I'm so caught off by the movement that I yelp in pure ecstasy and buck forward, wanting him deeper, wanting all of him.

Beck holds me back as he continues to drive into me, his arm muscles straining with his moments. "Look at how desperate they are," he whispers to me. "They are so close to the edge, wanted no one else but you on their laps. God, I love being me."

I'd been so wrapped up in my pleasure that I'd almost forgotten the crowd below me. Sure enough, everyone is on the edge of their seats. Even G.M. Fairy has her dress hiked up, her fingers deep inside her. Winston's pants are pulled down, his cock erect and tall. He strokes it with such slow moments, not letting his eyes drift from me. I make eye contact with him as Beck continues to pump his fingers into me. I almost lose myself. It's like I'm being fucked by everyone in the audience simultaneously, the pleasure they're experiencing mixing in with mine.

Beck pulls his fingers out of me and drags them up and down my cunt, circling at my clit. His lap is soaked underneath me.

I grab his neck and pull my face towards him, capturing his lips.

He fondles my breasts with one hand, alternating between jiggling them and pinching my nipples. His other hand focuses on my clit, bringing me right toward the edge.

I pull back from his lips. "I'm so close, baby."

"Come for us. We want to see your body writhe."

My body heeds his permission. I yell, my vocal cords straining as my body tightens and turns

to mush simultaneously. "Fuck, so good," I moan as the last of my orgasm washes through me.

I look back to the crowd as I catch my breath. Some people are using tissues to clean themselves up. They must have timed themself to match me. But the show's not over. In a second, my nerves are on fire, ready for more. The Gumdrop Buttons Winston gave us are doing their job. It doesn't have to do much, though. This whole scenario is so erotic that I could probably continue to come without it. Not to mention my hunk of an ogre behind me, using one arm to hold me up while working on unbuttoning his slacks.

The crowd looks ready for more as well. Their mouths are watering for me. Soft moans and the flash of movements flash all around me.

I lean back against Beck, using my feet still on the seat to push myself up to give him room to pound into me, already missing the presence of his body.

Beck pulls his pants down his legs, his cock hard and dripping.

I position myself to sit down on him, but he stops me, holding my body close to his chest. "Not yet, baby. Don't you want to show everyone how you're such a good girl? Show them how you use that pretty little mouth of yours."

His words send shivers down my spine, and my mouth waters thinking about his taste. I was so eager to have him inside of me. I didn't even think that I could drag this out and have even more fun.

I slide down his body, fall to my knees and face him. My black dress is scrunched up to my middle and I slowly pull the full thing over my head and throw it to the crowd. I turn back to see who caught it. Of course, it's Winston, as if he has a charm working in his favor. He gives me a wink as he brings the fabric to his nose, breathing it in and then letting his head fall back. He removes his hand from himself and grips his armrests as if my scent is all too much.

I turn back to Beck, catching his dark, heated stare. He watches my movements as if I'm some exotic creature he's never seen before. I slowly run my hands down his thighs, rubbing my breasts on his dick. I love the way his breath hitches from just my simple touch. I grab the base of him, and he groans, bucking his hips slightly. I run my hand up his length, luxuriating in his size, imagining him deep inside me. I lick my lips before lapping up the drops of pre-cum at his tip. "God, you taste so good." I look up at him, clenching his armrests, his neck strained as if it's taking everything in him not to blow his load all over my face already.

A devilish thought comes to me. I want to make him come, hard and fast. I know he's using everything in him to hold back, but I want to make that much harder for him. God, I love being a brat.

I lick his length, drooling on him when I get to his tip before pumping my hand up and down.

"Slow down," he growls.

I smirk at him, his dick in my hand. "No," I say before I take all of him in my mouth, gagging once I get to his base.

"Fuck," he cries as I use my hand and my mouth to take every inch of him inside of me. He gently tugs my hair, but I don't give up. I continue my speed, slobbering all over him, taking him in as far as he can go.

He pulls harder, but I persist, loving the pain of him pulling my hair. I strain against his grip, but he continues pulling harder until I almost can't take it. "Naughty girl," he groans before losing himself, letting go of my hair and pounding into me. My eyes water as he repeatedly hits the back of my throat until he comes undone. A warmness floods my mouth, and I lap him up eagerly, but I don't get to take my time because, within seconds, he grabs my arm, pulling me over his lap. He brings his hand down against my bare ass, the sound vibrating through the room.

I cry out, the sting of his slap igniting every nerve in my body.

"Bad girls get punished." His hand comes down upon me again; this time, my yelp is more subdued. I can already feel his hand marks forming on my ass. The thought of seeing his mark thrills me. It must thrill him too, because I feel him harden underneath my belly.

"Punish me with your dick," I cry.

He gives a low chuckle. "You'd like that, wouldn't you?"

"Yes." I'm too afraid to move. Too afraid that he won't give me what I want if I don't obey.

"On your knees," he orders.

I do as he says and pick myself up so I'm hovering over him, resting my hands and knees on the sides of the throne.

Beck grabs his hard cock, soaking wet from his fluids mixed with mine. "Now, I want you to sit down. Impale yourself with my dick."

"Yes," I moan, already eager to be so filled by him. I maneuver around and sit on his lap, his dick rubbing against my ass.

With one arm, Beck holds up my body. With the other, he positions his head at my entrance. He doesn't give me any warning before he thrusts into me.

My cries are louder than they've ever been. This is what I've been missing from the other orgasms. I've been craving his delicious length and to be so gloriously stuffed by him, feeling like any more could rip me in half.

He pounds into me as I bounce on his lap, my tits moving in a circular movement. I can barely keep my eyes open; the pleasure is too great to take in anything else, but I catch a glimpse of the crowd, wild and hungry for me.

Beck leans so his lips are to my ear. "Look at them. Look how wild you make them." He grabs my breast with one hand and my cunt with the other, flicking my clit in time with his thrusts.

"Fuck, it's so good," I yell, feeling so close to the edge again.

"Come with me, baby. Let's give them the grand finale." His voice is gruff and strained, sending shivers down my spine.

The music speeds up as if it's matching our performance. It only takes a few more pumps until we cry out, our bodies convulsing. I pulse around him, milking him for every last drop. Just as we begin to slack, the lights dim, the curtains pull around us, and the crowd quiets.

"Well, that was something," I say through my labored breath as I fall back against Beck.

Beck nods. He kisses my cheek and nuzzles my neck before whispering, "Best. Payment. Ever."

He's right. All of this seems too good to be true. Although I feel nothing but satisfaction right now, I can't help the creeping suspicion that this can't be it. Things can't be this easy.

CHAPTER THIRTEEN

Liona

"I can't believe I'm doing this," I whisper as I press the elevator button to the eleventh floor.

We've gone over the plan a thousand times. I just have to act casual, slip him the potion, and tell him to destroy all the evidence. G.M. Fairy told me the potion only lasts twenty-four hours, so unfortunately, I can't tell him to never try to find me again. I know there are so many things I could tell him to do, like jump out of his window, but I'm trying to keep this as mess-free as possible. If he doesn't have the evidence of Beck, he can't blackmail us. Sure, he knows where the magical community is, but if he attempted to come and get more evidence, well, it would be easier to dispose of him on our turf. I know there are holes in this plan, but I'm just trying to deal with one thing at a time. I just want to go back to my life, back to my swamp with my ogre, where we can live happily ever after.

Last night was a much-needed relief from the stress I've been under since receiving the letters from Lawrence. Even though going to the club was part of the plan to get me out of this marriage, it felt like an otherworldly vacation I needed. My body still feels the effects of the magnificent orgasms that rolled through me one after the other. I can't believe I even got out of bed this morning.

Luckily, I didn't run into Winston on my way out of the hotel. Beck and I left the club after our performance, but I think Winston stayed at Happily Ever Endings until it closed.

I know I'll have to face him sooner or later. I just don't know how to act around him with everything that happened last night.

I take a breath as the elevator doors slide open. Just a few more steps until I'm at the door of Lawrence's penthouse suite.

It was a struggle to convince Beck to let me go alone. He'd changed back into his human form before we left the club, but it didn't mean he was human enough to meet with Lawrence. He's a monster for God's sake. He'd probably rip his face off the second he saw him. Luckily, he was in a pleasant mood from all our fun last night. But I knew this pleasant mood would be nothing if Beck met Lawrence face to face. It would have gotten too messy too fast. I have to do this on my own.

I walk up to Lawrence's door and knock, my heart beating out of my chest as I wait for him to open it.

"Liona, it's so great to see you!" Lawrence says, smiling as soon as he opens the door. He's wearing a baby blue polo shirt and khaki slacks. He looks as stupid as I remembered, and it takes everything in me not to barf all over him.

I don't say anything, just walk past him into his apartment. The apartment that I used to call home. The apartment that he fucks his sister in. I hold back my barf once again.

"I'm glad you finally decided to be reasonable about this. I was elated this morning when you called and said you wanted to meet," he says, walking before me to the living room. "Have a seat." He motions to the chair across from a coffee table.

I hesitate for a second, my arms crossed over my chest.

"Come on, Liona. We were together for a long time. I won't bite. We have wedding plans to discuss."

Remember why you're here. Remember why you're here, I repeat in my head as I sit.

Lawrence sits on the couch parallel to me, lounging back with his arm on the armrest. "Is there anything I can get you first?"

Yes. My plan depends on this question. Lawrence may be many horrible things, but at least he's always a gracious host. "I'd love some tea." I cross my legs and straighten my skirt, trying to remain cool.

"Of course, I know how you always loved your tea." He heads to the kitchen, clacking in his cabinets. "So, how are you enjoying your stay? Do you miss LA?" he calls from the kitchen.

I fidget with the bottle in my pocket. Feeling its presence calms my nerves and keeps me from lashing out in anger. "Yeah, sure," I reply.

Lawrence walks back into the living room with a teapot, two small glasses, and a small container of cream, all balanced on a silver tray. He puts the tray down in front of me. "There we are."

I grab my teacup and place his in front of his seat. "Can I have some sugar?"

"Sugar?" He looks down at me, still standing with his hands on his hips. "But you never liked sugar in your tea before."

I begin pouring the tea into both of our cups. "Well, people change. There are many different things I like now." I hold his gaze.

His eyes dart, and he fidgets, clearly unnerved by my confidence. "Okay then. I'll go get you some sugar." The second he disappears back in the kitchen, I yank off the cork lid of the potion and dump it into his tea, praying to all the gods in the universe that it doesn't have a weird smell that he'll notice.

"So, I thought we'd have a private ceremony at Mother's in two days. That way the family lawyer can quickly oversee the marriage certificate, and we can get this inheritance nonsense out of the way." He walks back into the living room, barely giving me a second to spare before I put the empty container back in my pocket and can blow on my tea to appear casual. That was a close one, and my heart hammers in my chest.

"Why not just at the courthouse?" I ask before taking the sugar from him and dumping a spoonful of it into my tea. I take a sip and try to hide my distaste. I still fucking hate sugar in my tea.

Even though this is all a ruse, discussing marriage with this prick kills me. He's put such a sour taste in my mouth for the whole wedding ordeal, and it's unfair to Beck. And me.

Lawrence sits down and takes a big gulp of his tea.

I watch him, wondering how long it will take to go into effect.

"I'd rather not have the possibility of random people ruining our day. It can be quick and easy in the privacy of my family." He takes another sip of his tea and then pauses. "You know what. If you want to have it at the courthouse, let's do it there!" He grins, even giddier than his usual bullshit smile.

Maybe this is it. Maybe the potion is already working. I need to test it out first. "Lawrence, could you give me a hundred dollars? I'm running low on cash."

"Of course!" He jams his hand into his pocket and pulls out his wallet as if he's more than eager to heed my request. "Here you go." He hands me a crisp hundred-dollar bill. It must be working. Even when Lawrence was supplying my life, he always gave me grief whenever I asked for anything outside my weekly allowance. Now he's just handing over hundies like a mother fucking jolly Monopoly man. Time to pull out the big guns.

"Lawrence, I want you to do something for me. Do you think you could do that?"

"Yes, of course, whatever you want." His eyes hold a doe-like quality, and he looks even more brain-dead than usual.

No turning back now. "I want you to destroy all the evidence, and I mean all, of Beck being an ogre, and I want you to get rid of anything you have written down about where the magical community is." I know he will still know where it's located, but I doubt he remembers the address from memory. I shouldn't get any letters anytime soon if this works.

He's still for a moment—the stupid smile remains on his face. "Okay!" he exclaims cheerfully before getting up from his seat and walking down the hallway.

I put down my tea and follow him. I want to see just how much he's actually got on us.

He leads me to his office. The office that I was never allowed in before. Of course, I've always been a rebellious brat, so I'd sneaked in here a few times, but it never seemed worth my while. It was just a normal office with boring files in boring filing cabinets.

Lawrence heads straight to a large armoire and opens it to reveal several of his blazers hanging. He pushes them to the side and steps inside.

I lean closer to see him type in numbers on a keypad at the back of the wardrobe. The keypad beeps, and the wall slides open.

"You have to be shitting me." Has Lawrence had a secret room all this time? How did I not know the apartment I'd lived in for years had a secret room? Knowing how fucked up Lawrence is, I'm absolutely terrified to find what he has hidden back here, but there's no time to be scared. I follow him into the dark secret passageway.

Lawrence flicks the lights to reveal a sterile room lined with filing cabinets. A huge monitor and computers are situated at a long desk at the very end of the room.

I should have known that his secret room would be as boring and lifeless as him. I honestly wish he had body parts tacked to the walls just to make this more interesting.

"What is this place?" I ask.

"Oh, it's just my blackmail room. There are many benefits to owning so many of the security systems in LA. I have information about all my friends, family, and everyone even remotely important. You must stay prepared."

"Do you have shit on Victoria?" I can't help but ask.

"Yep."

I sigh. "Of course you do." I don't know how he could have anything worse on her than the fact that she's fucking him, her brother, but I guess completely vile people have a never-ending list of horrible shit they commit.

"Okay, so let's get rid of all the information on Beck and me."

"Yes!" Lawrence says as he heads to a filing cabinet to his left.

As I follow, I notice that the row is labeled "L." He opens the drawer and takes out a giant file with my name neatly typed on the front.

"Is that whole thing shit you have on me?"

"We were together for a long time. You're my biggest file. Well, besides Mother's."

What a fucking sociopath. "Okay, let's destroy it."

"No problem!" He carries it over to a large shredder and drops it in.

I know I just found out about his fucked-up filing system, but I swear I feel a mountain lift off my shoulder once I hear those papers shred to bits. "Is that all of it?" I ask.

Lawrence laughs. "No, silly. I have everything backed up on my hard drive."

"Delete it," I bark.

"Okie dokie." Lawrence skips over to his computer.

I can't help but laugh to myself at how utterly ridiculous he looks.

He types in a password a few times and pulls up a file hidden within another file. He clicks on the folder with my name. Images, videos, and text files completely cover every inch of the screen. Man, does he have a lot of shit on me. I didn't know I had this much to be blackmailed with. "Delete all of it, now, and then delete it from your trash. Make sure there is no trace of any files that have to do with me, my ogre, or anything in the magical community."

"You got it!"

I watch as he deletes everything, going to different files as he deletes more and more. He also has a separate folder dedicated to just the magical community, which he deletes. "Alrighty, it's all done." He looks back and smiles at me.

"Good." My brain is racing. I'm pissed. I can't believe Lawrence had violated my privacy so much throughout our relationship. I'd caught glimpses of videos and pictures of me in the shower, picking my nose, and even masturbating. I knew he was an incestual douchebag, but God damn, is he fucked up. It's not fair that his only punishment for being so evil is not getting *all* of his inheritance from his dead father. I know I might regret this later, but there needs to be consequences for his actions.

"Do you have files about you and Victoria's relation-ship?"

His smile doesn't leave his face. "Yes, of course. You never know when you just want to watch the world burn."

Okay, this charming spell is getting a little creepy.

"I want you to post all of it, but only videos and pictures you're both in. Post it everywhere and send it to every major news outlet."

He freezes for a second, his smile fading.

Shit. I've gone too far. The potion must be wearing off.

"Okay!" he finally exclaims, the smile reappearing on his face.

I breathe out and watch as he opens files with videos of Victoria and him making out, role-playing as animals, tying each other up, and fucking each other in every way possible. I turn around and barf on the floor, unable to contain myself anymore. "Just send all of it!" I yell in be-tween gags.

"One second." He hits some more buttons on his com-puter. "Done! Anything else you need?"

I wipe my mouth with the back of my hand and glare at him, sitting in his office chair, staring back at me with a complacent grin.

Shit. I didn't realize how bad the files were. I've got to get out of here. When this potion wears off, I'm going to be in trouble.

Chapter Fourteen

Beck

I'm sure I'm leaving marks on the floor from my insistent pacing.

"Calm down. She's going to be fine. She can handle herself," Winston says from the chair in the corner of our room.

"I shouldn't have let her go alone. I don't care if she thinks I can't contain myself. At least she would be safe," I growl back at him.

We haven't addressed the elephant in the room — everything that happened last night at the club — and I'd like to keep it that way. What's done is done. I fucked Liona in front of him. He jacked himself off to it. What more is there to say?

"She'll be fine. She has the potion. Relax."

I stop treading, turn around, and snarl at him, ready to take out my anxiety on him, but just then, someone fidgets with the door key from the other side.

Liona. All my thoughts turn to her, and I run to the door, yanking it open before the person on the other side even has a chance to try.

"Oh!" she startles. "I..."

I don't let her finish before I wrap my arms around her, pick her up, and carry her into the room. "Are you okay?" I ask once I put her down on the ground and run my hands up her body, looking for any indication of injury.

She laughs, her eyes sparkling with the delight of my concern. God, I can't let this beautiful woman out of my sight again.

"I'm fine." She cups my face, smiling at me, but then her face turns downward. "But we need to go. Like now."

"Did everything go according to plan?" Winston asks, walking toward us.

Her eyes shift between us, and she fidgets with the ends of her hair. "Sort of. I mean, yes. The Charming Potion worked, and I got him to delete all the blackmail, but...."

"But what?" I ask, not able to wait for another second. God, if he touched her, I swear I will burn down this whole city.

"I kind of got carried away." A red hue lines her tanned cheeks.

"Meaning?" Winston steps closer, searching her face.

She puts her face in her hands. "I made him send out all the evidence of Victoria and his relationship."

I chuckle and reach for a high-five. "Nice!"

Liona just looks at me and shakes her head. "No, not nice. Sure, it felt good, but now Lawrence will get revenge. The potion only lasts twenty-four hours. When it wears off, he's coming for my head."

Winston scrolls through his phone. "Buying tickets now for the red eye tonight."

Liona's shoulders relax, and she breathes out a sigh of relief. "Thank you. I think once we get back home, everything will feel better."

Seeing Liona calm down calms me as well. I know she's worried that Lawrence could do something to her while she's still here, but she's got nothing to worry about. As long as she's with me, she's safe.

I reach out and pull her into my arms. I know it's selfish. I know she just got out of one marriage and probably doesn't want to think about another, but I can't help but wonder if now is a good time to bring the subject up again. I just want every part of her and won't be satisfied until she's all mine.

But before I can bring up anything, Liona pulls back. "I think I'm gonna throw up." She rushes towards the bathroom and slams the door behind her. It's like she can tell when I'm even thinking about marriage and becomes physically ill. I can't be frustrated at her, though. She can't help it.

I walk over and gently tap on the door. "Everything okay?"

"Yeah," she says in between gags. "Just give me a minute."

I turn to Winston, and we both shrug.

"Well, I hope she feels better before tonight. That would suck to have to take such a long flight while sick."

"Yeah. She got sick like this last week and got over it pretty quickly. I think it's the whole Lawrence situation. Every time she thinks about marrying him, she vomits."

"Understandable." He walks towards the door. "I'm going to try to get some sleep before our flight tonight. Let me know if you need anything." He turns before exiting. "Good job these past few days. I could see a real future in the performing industry for you two." He winks and shuts the door.

Such a freak.

I sigh and knock on the bathroom door. "Can I get you anything?"

"Maybe a ginger ale?" She sounds pitiful, and I hate that she's feeling sick again. I can't believe this prick has such a negative effect on her. I wish I could get rid of him the good old fashion way. I may even give up my human fast just for him.

"Yeah, I'll be right back." At least I can do this simple task for her. If only that could be enough.

***

The ice cubes in the ginger ale I got from the bar downstairs clack together as the elevator stops at the top floor. I wait for the doors to roll open, mentally preparing myself for another six-hour flight in the middle of the night. Liona and I got home late last night, and she was up early, messaging Lawrence about their meeting. I was up when she was up and couldn't even sit still the moment she left. Hopefully, Liona won't be too sick, and we can rest once this ginger ale settles in her stomach.

I turn down the hallway and walk up to our door. It's open.

Dread drops like an atomic bomb in my stomach. I barge in to find the room completely ransacked. The furniture is turned over, and the sheets are ripped off the bed.

"Liona!" I yell, banging open the bathroom door.

But she's gone. He took her.

CHAPTER FIFTEEN

Beck

"She's gone! We need to find her." I barge into Winston's room before he even has a second to open the door fully.

"What? What do you mean she's gone? I was just with you guys?"

"I know, but I went to get her ginger ale, and when I returned, the room was ransacked, and she was gone. Fuck! Just help me find her. Can you do the spell that helped me find her last time she ran away from the swamp?" I'm pacing around Winston's room, pulling at my hair.

"Yes, yes. Okay. Calm down." He rushes to his closet and pulls out a leather briefcase. "I just don't understand why he would take her. The charm isn't supposed to wear off for a while," he says as he rummages through his bag, pulling out a map, a clear crystal hanging on a rope, a piece of hair, and a vial full of iridescent powder.

I remember this ritual from the last time I asked him to track her down. "You still have the piece of her hair I gave you?"

"I'm always prepared. I wasn't about to come here without a safeguard in case everything went to shit."

I should be creeped out, but I don't give a fuck. I'm just thankful he has a way to find her.

He lays the map out on his bed, pours the powder over the top, sprinkles her hair, and dangles the crystal over it. The crystal moves, at first looking as if Winston is just swinging it to his whim, but then it becomes more frantic, pulling him down to a point on the map. The map changes; instead of revealing a sketch of the United States, it zooms in, revealing a more detailed location.

"Where is she?" I ask, pushing myself closer to examine the changing image.

"I'm not sure yet. It's not done calculating. But I know she's alive. It wouldn't keep zoning in if she wasn't."

Some of my nerves melt away. At least I can save her, but dread still fills me because I know that being alive and safe are two entirely different things.

Finally, an image of Liona tied to a chair in a dark room is illuminated over the map. Her body is slack, and her head hangs limply against her shoulder.

"Liona!" I yell, reaching through the image. Any rational thought about the possibility of actually retrieving her this way has escaped me.

"Beck, calm down," Winston says, pushing my hand back. "Let me read where she is." His eyes scan over the words next to the image of her. It's not written in a language I understand. It must be some magical wizard script.

"Okay, I know where she is, but I can imagine it will be difficult to get in."

"I don't fucking care. Show me where she is, and I'll rip everyone's head off in the vicinity until I get to her."

"You're going to need your ogre strength. This human form you're in mutes some of your abilities."

"Then fucking give me the antidote. Let's stop talking about it and get to her."

"Okay, okay. Let me just get some other potions and my wand. I can use my powers to help as well." He rushes back to his closet, pulls out different vials and a long wand, and shoves them into his pocket. "Okay. I'm ready."

I charge through his door, ready to run to the location if necessary. "Good. Time to fuck some shit up."

***

The black car Winston called for us rolls up to the empty warehouse on the city's outskirts.

"Are you sure this is where you want me to drop you two off?" asks the driver, facing us.

"Yes, and I want you to leave this place and forget that you brought us here." Winston waves his wand in front of the driver, and his face transforms into a blank stare.

"Of course," he says before getting out and opening the door for us.

"You can make people forget things without your memory loss potion?" I ask as Winston, and I walk to the warehouse. This trip took several hours to arrive, so thankfully, we're shaded by the dimming sun.

"Yes, but only if the thing I'm making them forget is a small occurrence."

"Magic is weird," I huff.

"Agreed."

We crouch low behind a tree before we get too close to the warehouse.

"Okay, so what's the plan?" I whisper.

"What do you mean, what's the plan? I thought you had a plan. You were the one who rushed us out here."

"You always have a plan," I bark.

"Well, I don't have one now, so what are we going to do?"

I ponder for a moment. I've never been good at scheming or coming up with bright ideas. I have the brawn, not the brains. I finally say and shrug my shoulders. "Fuck shit up?"

Winston sighs as well. "Fuck shit up." He hands me the potion. "Use this when you need to."

I nod, taking it from him and shoving it in my pocket before barreling towards the warehouse, caution completely leaving me.

Winston charges behind me, a low growl at the back of his throat.

Here goes nothing.

Chapter Sixteen

Liona

"Fuck." My head pounds, my neck is on fire, and my wrists and ankles are sore. My puffy eyes require a second for me to take in my surroundings. "Where am I?" I ask no one in particular. I'm alone in a dark, desolate room. The only sounds around me are drips of water droplets and creaking pipes. I look down. "Shit." I'm tied to a metal chair, my feet bound to the legs, and my arms are secured behind my back.

My memory floods with what I remember last. I was back at the hotel, throwing up in the bathroom, when two men charged in and fought to tie me up. I struggled, trying to take the whole room with me, but I was eventually knocked out. How can this be? The potion shouldn't have worn off so soon. Lawrence shouldn't realize what I did yet. I thought we'd be safe until we could return to our swamp.

"Well, well, well, you finally woke up," a voice calls from down a dark hallway to my side.

I recognize this voice.

Bouncy, blonde curls crown the angular face of the person I'd thought I'd never have to see again. She walks closer to me, her heels tapping against the concrete floor.

"Victoria, what do you want?" I roll my eyes. This bitch? This bitch really wants to try me?

"Do you think you could try to ruin my life without any consequences?"

I guess I hadn't considered that Victoria could seek revenge for me leaking her and her brother's incestual affair, but what the fuck is she going to do? Decorate me to death? Talk shit about me until I die? But now that she has me tied up to a chair in some creepy ass warehouse, I guess I should reconsider her abilities. Obviously, she has the money to hire the men who kidnapped me and will probably kill me. I would have never guessed she had it in her.

I sigh. "Victoria, this has nothing to do with you. Lawrence was blackmailing me to marry him. He had all this shit on me and even more on you. I'm sorry that I ruined your life, but don't you think you kind of deserved it? You were pretending to be my best friend while fucking my fiancé—your brother!"

"Don't act so innocent." She pulls up a stool and sits in from of me, her blue eyes dark with anger. She's wearing black leather pants and a tiny black tank top. Definitely not anything I've ever seen her in. What is she trying to be, some sexy villain right now? I suppress my snarky remarks.

"Do you think I don't know you were fucking a monster when you ran away from your bachelorette party? Do you think you're so innocent of accusing me of being a mistress with your fiancé? Do you really think you hold the compass on morality? Your lover isn't even the same species as you."

"Yes, but he's still not my brother. Don't pretend you don't win the most fucked up award."

She smacks me across my cheek.

I must admit it stings. Those Pilates must be doing something.

"I'd watch that mouth of yours. You are tied up with no way to get out." She crosses her legs and examines her shiny red nails.

"Let's cut to the chase. What do you want, Victoria?

She leans in closer. "I want you to marry Lawrence."

"What? Why? Don't you want to be with him?"

She chuckles, stands up, and paces around me. "Look at you, such a romantic," she says mockingly. "Lawrence and I's relationship is purely physical. You wouldn't understand, but I've always wanted you two to be married. I'm not stupid. I know you never loved him, and I know you came from nothing. You're the perfect choice. You could live the life of your dreams and stay out of our way."

I shake my head, feeling bile rise from my throat again from thinking about them together.

"Just let him stay single so you two can have your money and your privacy. Leave me out of it."

"Stop acting stupid!" she yells, a crazy look in her eyes as she leans in close. "You know that Lawrence doesn't get the full inheritance unless he's married. It's too complicated to find another wife who would try to mess up what we have. We had blackmail on you. You're the perfect choice."

"Well now you don't, so find someone else." I spit in her face.

She startles and pulls back, wiping my spit off with the back of her hand. She takes a deep breath and then punches me in the jaw.

"Fuck!" I yell, spitting out blood.

She leans in close again and grabs me by the shoulders. "Well, now you pissed me off. It's personal. Sure, my PR person can make all the messiness you tried to cause disappear, but you must be punished for what you did. Now, if you ever want to leave this warehouse, you're going to marry Lawrence, whenever whatever magical spell you put on him fades, which I know it will because it's already seeming to lessen."

"You're crazy! Are you really going to go through all the trouble of kidnapping me and keeping me here until I marry your brother? It would be so much easier to find someone else!"

"Maybe I am crazy, but I'm not in the business of doing things because they're easier. You pissed me off, and now you pay."

A door bangs open from the far end of the room. "Ms. Farque, we have visitors," says a gruff voice.

Both of our heads snap to the source.

Victoria walks forward, catching a glimpse of whoever entered before I can. "Well, well, well, it looks like your two little pets attempted to save you. How sad that they didn't get very far."

Five burly men walk into the center of the room, each over six feet tall. In their grasps are Beck, in his human form, and Winston.

"Beck!" I yell.

He yanks against the three men holding him back and pulls away, but the men charge at him and bound his arms behind his back in seconds.

"I must say, I don't know how you got your ogre to look so human. The last disguise was pretty pathetic." She laughs and pinches his cheek.

Beck growls and attempts to bite her fingers.

"Oh, a feisty one. I can see why you like him." She walks over to Winston.

"And who do we have here? Did you bring in a third?" She walks around him but glances in my direction.

"Leave them alone. I'll marry Lawrence if you just let them go!" I yell. All I wanted was to get this over with without putting the people I love at risk. I don't know how it got so messy with all of us captured in a warehouse. I should have just married Lawrence in the first place instead of fucking things up and trying to get revenge.

"That option is over now, sweet cheeks." She yawns. "Tie them up. Now that we don't have blackmail to hold over her, it will be easier for us to get her to do what we want if we torture them in front of her."

"No!" I yell, struggling against my binds.

She ignores me. "I'm done here. I need to check on Lawrence and make sure he hasn't given away our whole estate. Save the fun for me later, though. You boys good here?" She flips her hair over her shoulder and saunters down the hallway where she came from.

"Yes, ma'am," one of the brute men replies, but Victoria is already out of sight, and a door slams shut. She's gone.

"Let's tie them to this pillar," says one of the men.

They push Beck and Winston back, getting them halfway across the warehouse before Winston yells, "One, two, three!"

Beck pulls away from his three captors. He must have been pretending he was weaker to get them to take him to me. He pulls a vial out of his pocket and chugs it in one gulp. In a flash, Beck is transformed from his human form back into an ogre, his shirt ripping off his green chiseled body.

The three men charge at him, but Beck drops to his knees and slides toward them, knocking them off their feet. He jumps up and runs toward the men holding Winston, punching them both in the jaw, one after the other. They're knocked back, letting Winston escape their grips.

In a flash, Winston pulls out his wand and directs it to one of the men, instantly freezing him in place. The only part of his body not frozen are his eyes shifting back and forth.

It's all happening so fast, I can barely keep up.

The other four men gawk at their frozen counterparts, giving Beck the time to grab one of them and snap his neck in one swift motion. The man drops to the floor.

I just sit in my binds, feeling useless. I tug against them even though I know it's futile. But honestly, watching Beck kill a man with his bare hands sends a rush of warmth to my core. I'm brought back to when Beck fucked me in Donny's blood. I could stay right where I am for a while, although I'd rather be able to touch myself while I watch.

With a slight hesitation, the other three men charge at Beck.

From behind, Winston points his hand at one of the men, and he freezes in his steps.

Beck runs towards the two men left, still charging at him, with his arms out wide. The men slam into Beck's outstretched arms and fall onto their backs.

Beck falls to his knees and drops his fists onto their faces. Their blood splatters across Beck's face and chest. He hits them three more times in rapid succession, making more and more blood splatter onto him. He doesn't stop until the men are completely still.

The room is silent. Two men are still frozen, and the other three lie on the floor dead.

Beck looks down at the two by him, catching his breath, but then looks up at me, his eyes dark and his face serious. He picks himself up and starts towards me.

"Beck!" I yell.

"Liona." He gives a relieved sob before reaching me. He captures my lips with his, running his hands through my hair, desperation from him filling me.

I pull on my binds, wanting to grab him with the same intensity he's grabbing me.

He falls to his knees and gives an animalistic grunt as he rips the ropes securing my legs to the chairs. He stands up and does the same to the ropes on my arms.

The second my arms are free, I grab him, pulling his neck down to meet my lips.

He grabs my waist with one hand and my ass with the other, sweeping me up in his arms. I wrap my legs around him, clinging to all of him. He sits in the chair, ripping off my flimsy white shirt, now covered in blood.

I can't think straight. I'm like a bull who's seen red. Everything in me just needs him inside of me.

He must feel the same way because he yanks down his pants, never letting his mouth leave mine. His manhood presses against me, demanding I make way. Luckily, I'm still wearing a skirt, and I can push it to the side, giving him access to me. I'm not wearing underwear. I never wear underwear. I'm a slut, and I love it.

Within seconds I'm holding onto Beck's neck, picking up my hips and moaning into his ear as he adjusts himself at my entrance. Just his tip is inside of me until I use all my force to impale myself onto him, my wet cunt welcoming him eagerly. We both cry out.

"Um, guys. Shouldn't we get out of here?"

Shit. I forgot about Winston.

I stop my movements and try to turn to address him.

Beck grabs my hips, picks them up, and slams into me again, causing me to cry out. "Fuck off, Winston. Just give us a few seconds."

He wants me—*needs*—me so bad that he doesn't give a shit if Winston's in the room or if we barely have seconds before the next set of henchmen come in to tie us up again. God, he's so fucking hot.

I surrender myself to him, bouncing up and down on his lap as he holds onto me like I'm seconds away from slipping from his fingers.

"I love you!" I cry.

"I love you too," he growls back.

In just a few more thrusts, we both reach our edge. We cry out. I pulse around him, milking him for every last drop.

I collapse onto his chest, and he runs his hands down my back. "We got to stop doing this. You know how hard it is to get blood out of clothes?" I look down at the blood smears on my skirt.

I feel his lips form into a smile from my words.

Winston claps. "You two sure do love to put on a show. Now if you're both done, can we get the fuck out of here? We have a plane to catch."

I get off Beck's lap and hold my breasts while Beck yanks up his pants and adjusts the buttons. I'm suddenly aware that Beck has just ripped my shirt off, and I might have to leave this place topless.

"Here you go," Winston says as he walks closer to us. "Take this." He pulls off his white button down and hands it to me.

Pulling the shirt on, I glance at the three of us. Beck and Winston are now shirtless, I don't think anyone would complain about that, but we're also all covered in blood and dirt. "I don't think they're letting us onto the plane like this."

Winston looks at his watch. "If we leave now, I can call a cab, and we can clean up at the hotel before we have to leave for our flight, but it's going to be tight." He reaches into his pocket and takes out a vial. "You'll need to change back into a human before we leave here, or all of this will be for nothing."

"Right," Beck says before removing the top and chugging it. He's more used to the transition now. He just closes his eyes and rubs his temple as he transforms into a human. Seeing his beautiful green skin switch back to a human beige is unnerving.

After a few seconds, he picks up his head. "Let's get the fuck out of here and back to the swamp."

CHAPTER SEVENTEEN

Beck

It's been two weeks since we arrived back in the magical community. I sometimes wake in the dead of night, sure that Victoria and Lawrence's henchmen are barging through our door to capture Liona again. But nothing has happened. There's no more blackmail. What else can the two of them do besides show up here? I think they both know that would be a vast mistake, regardless of how much power and resources they have. We have an army of terrifying creatures that could instantly make them disappear.

Winston has been working on barrier spells to shield our community even more as an extra precaution. They still aren't perfect, so on rare occasions we get a straggler and give them the memory loss potion and send them on their way. But he's been working diligently since we've returned, and the results have been promising. I must say, he's a talented wizard, and even though I think he can be a bit of a freak, he's a good friend, maybe the best I've ever had. I would have never thought I could be friends with someone who enjoyed watching me fuck Liona, but who can blame him? Who wouldn't want to see that?

I'm not stupid. I know this probably won't be the last time we hear from the Farques, but for now, we're safe.

Liona and I have barely left our cottage since we returned home. There's been a hungry need to keep each other to ourselves. Today, we've decided it would be good to get out of the house and take a swim in the spring nearby. The sun shines through the canopy of leaves, and the birds sing off in the distance. Liona floats in the water naked, her eyes closed as she welcomes the rays of sunlight that kiss her soft tanned skin.

I can't help but stare at her, soaking in the beauty that always takes my breath away. I think about that feeling when I discovered her taken or saw her tied up in that warehouse, and my insides turn to molten lava. I vow to never let her out of my sight again. I was able to protect her, but I was so close to losing her.

I extend my arms and grab her.

She gives a tiny shriek but then softens and welcomes my embrace.

I kiss her cheek. "Are you happy to be back home?" She hasn't indicated that she misses LA, but I can't fight the images of seeing her light up at the restaurants, the shops, and the club. She liked being around so many people like herself. Whether she admits it or not, I know there is a part of her life before me that my solitude could never replace.

She looks at me and wraps her legs around me. "Of course. There's no place I'd rather be."

Feeling her naked body pressed against mine sends a surge of electricity through me, and I feel my cock harden, even though I'd just been inside of her an hour earlier. I run my hand through her silky wet hair, wanting to savor this still and peaceful moment together.

I haven't brought up marriage again. I know that now the messiness with Lawrence is over, she might say yes, but I don't think I could stomach another refusal. What if it was never about Lawrence in the first place? What if she doesn't want to be married because she doesn't want to feel tied down to this place—to me?

She must notice how my inner thoughts run rampant because she looks up at me and asks, "What are you thinking about?"

I sigh. "Just us."

"Us?" She smirks and swims back a bit. "Do you mean us fucking in this spring? Because that's what I'm thinking about."

If I was hard before, now I'm absolutely rigid. I swim after her.

She paddles away from me and screeches. She loves to play games. It's one of my favorite things about her.

I slow down, pretending she has a chance to outswim me until she gets to the shallow end of the spring, and I grab her ankle, pulling her into me.

Her scream is mixed with a laugh as I pull her body close, capturing her lips with mine. She squirms against me, but I hold her tight, not letting her get even an inch away from me. I grab her ass and rub her against my cock. She moans into my mouth as I slip a finger inside her, getting her ready for all of me.

She's dropped the ruse now and turns to grind against me, climbing up to position her entrance over me. I slide myself into her gently. I pull back, wanting to watch as I fuck her. Her eyes close as she cries in ecstasy.

I stop thrusting into her. "Open your eyes or I'll stop. I want to look into you."

Her eyes flutter open, and we maintain eye contact, but it takes everything in both of us to keep them open, the pleasure rolling through us and dragging us under.

I could stare into her eyes forever. The deep blue that puts this body of water to shame carries me to an unearthly place. I stare into her as I drive myself deeper and deeper inside her, our bodies becoming one as we get closer and closer to the inevitable edge. I never want this to end. When our orgasms roll over us and I slip out of her, I will just be counting the seconds until I can be part of her again. I wonder if marriage could fill this void. I know it's just a custom, a demonstration passed down, but it feels like the last frontier for us. I don't think marriage would ever make the need to drive myself into her less urgent, but maybe it could calm my spirit even a little.

She pulses around me, the sensation bringing me to my end—spilling into her. I don't let go of her. If anything, I grab onto her more, savoring every touch, every breath against my neck as she settles herself. We just let the water drag us back and forth—nothing matters except us.

"Beck," she whispers, her voice shaky.

"Yes."

"Ask me again."

"What?" I pull her back to search her face.

"Ask me again."

I know what she means but can't believe what I hear. I don't question it, though. I swim to the shore and rummage through my shorts' pockets, pulling out the little black box I always keep with me, just in case there is another perfect moment. I swim back to her, flipping open the box to reveal the emerald ring. "Liona, will you marry me?"

Tears fall down her cheek. "Yes." She wraps her arms around me.

I can hardly believe my ears. I pull back. "Are you sure? I don't want to force you."

"Beck, I was sure the minute I fell in love with you. I don't think I'm good enough for you, but I guess you'll just have to forgive me for my shortcomings."

I laugh and slip the ring on her finger. "Not good enough for me? Liona, I'm an ogre."

She wraps her arms around my neck. "My life is a mess. I'm a mess, and I just wanted to sort my life out before I become fully yours. You are the most human man I have ever met. You're more than enough for me." She kisses me.

"You've always been mine. The minute you fell into my trap, you were mine."

"I know. I understand that now." She kisses me again. "Now, let's get married."

And just like that, life is perfect.

CHAPTER EIGHTEEN

Liona

Who knew wedding planning could actually be fun? Of course, the fact that I'm marrying the man of my dreams makes the whole experience wonderful. Still, weddings in the magical community are a big deal and I'm genuinely excited about the celebration.

I still can't believe I didn't say yes to Beck the first time he asked me. Of course, the fact that I had to marry Lawrence to make sure he didn't ruin all of our lives did put a gray cloud over the situation, but still, I should have said yes, regardless. I guess it's more on-brand for me to make him ask twice anyway. I do love the chase.

I've been to town every day this week. Beck and I will be married at our cottage in just two weeks, and although it will be low-key, there's so much to do.

As I walk through the busy streets, I can't help but notice the unusual number of smiles and waves I receive. The elf children can't suppress their giggles and whisper to each other as I pass them by. The young fox women blow me kisses. I do my best to return each gesture before turning it into the Clothing Shoppe.

"I was wondering when you would show up," Gilda, the Fairy Godmother shop owner, calls from the front counter before fluttering over to me. She wraps me in a hug.

After meeting G.M. Fairy, it's hard not to compare the two Fairy Godmothers. It's so odd how different they are. Sure, they're both older with grey hair and thin-framed glasses, but one runs a magical clothing boutique while the other runs a magical sex club. They couldn't be any more different.

I dismiss my thoughts. "I've just been so busy, I almost totally forgot about the dress."

Gilda gasps. "Forgot the dress? But that's the most important part! Come to the back, and let's get you the dress
of your dreams."

I follow her. "Everyone's been so nice to me since the
news spread about the wedding."

"Well, of course! You're the first human to be a part of
the community, and now you're getting married to Beck,
the community's fierce and solitary protector. It's quite
the story!" She snaps her fingers, and a tape measure appears, wrapping around my body on its own.

"Your measurements are a bit larger than last time, but
that's to be expected."

Oh shit. I guess I have liked Beck's cooking a little too
much lately. Back in LA, I would have been mortified to
know I'd gain weight for my wedding day, but now that
I'm with Beck, it doesn't matter. I know he'll love me
regardless. Although I would have preferred Gilda to keep
the news of my weight gain to herself.

"How are you feeling?" she asks as she flies around me,
reading the numbers of the tape measurer.

"I feel fine! Planning a wedding so quickly has made me a little more tired than usual, but I'm so excited that I don't mind."

"I bet that's not the only reason you feel tired." She chuckles to herself.

"Gilda!" I exclaim in surprise. Did Gilda just make a sex joke? Maybe she is more of a freak than I thought. I wonder if she would enjoy Happily Ever Endings. The thought of the club sends a chill down my spine. There are so many creatures in the community that would love that place. It's a shame they probably won't ever be able to experience it since they can't pass as humans.

I sigh and shake the naughty thoughts out of my head. "Yeah, I'm excited, but I'm kind of ready for it to be over so we can just relax with just us two."

"Twirl for me." Gilda removes a wand from her pocket and flicks her wrist. Fairy dust falls all around me, and I twirl as a white gown forms perfectly around my body. I look in the mirror at the satin, off-the-shoulder gown—a white flower crown forms on my head. I never knew what

I wanted to look like on my wedding day, but now I know—this is it. I've never been a sentimental person, but I feel tears welling in the corner of my eyes.

Gilda fidgets with my dress, inspecting the fabric from all angles. "You two won't have very long to relax. Babies don't usually allow for that."

"Babies?" I laugh. I know older people love to comment on this when a couple gets married, but I haven't even given babies a second thought. Sure, I've always wanted kids, but Beck and I aren't the same species. It's probably not even possible.

Gilda straightens and studies my face. "So, you're planning on just the one?" she asks tactfully.

"The one?" What is she talking about?

"Oh, my gods." She puts her hand on her chest. "You don't know?"

"Don't know what?"

She grabs my hands and stares deep into my eyes. "Liona, you're pregnant."

"Pregnant?" The world spins around me. "I'm not pregnant." Maybe a rumor has spread around the village, and everyone assumes this is a shotgun wedding.

"Oh, dear. Come sit down." She leads me to a chair. "I assumed you knew since you're quite far along. As a Fairy Godmother, I can sense these things."

My heart hammers out of my chest, and I clutch my stomach. I think back to the last few months. The mood swings, the throwing up, and now that I think about it, I haven't gotten my period in a while. Oh, God.

"How far along am I?"

Gilda puts a hand on my stomach. "You're almost five months, and you've got a healthy baby in there. Oh goodness, I can't wait to see how cute a half-ogre half-human baby is!"

"How is this possible?"

"Well, I don't think I need to explain that to you, but..."

"No, I mean, how is it possible for Beck and me to have a baby together? We're not the same species."

She shrugs. "Magic is a mysterious thing."

I sigh and slump back against my chair. "That's for sure." It seems like every day magic becomes even more and more confusing. I can't untangle my thoughts. Of course, I'm excited, but I also didn't expect this. Now I only have four more months to prepare before this baby comes. Most importantly, I need to tell Beck, like right now.

I stand up. "I've got to go." I start toward the door but stop before I push it open, realizing I'm still wearing my dress. I turn back to face Gilda. She just smiles and snaps her fingers. The dress disappears from my body, and the clothes I arrived in return.

She smiles. "Go on now. I'll have the dress ready for you on your wedding day. Go and get your man."

***

"Shit!" I yell after bumping my shin on the bench in front of Beck and I's bed. I've been pacing for fifteen minutes, considering how I should tell Beck we're having a baby. Should I do something cute, like bake a bun and tell him to look in the oven? No. He'll be back any minute from hunting, and I'm a shit baker.

This moment is much too monumental just to come out and tell him. I need to be cleverer and think of something he will remember and cherish forever.

As if the universe replies with a big, "fuck you and your plans," the front door opens. "I'm home," Beck announces as he walks through the threshold.

"Shit!" I mean to say it in my head but say it out loud. Pregnancy brain.

"Um, should I just leave and never come back?" He points toward the direction he came from.

He's so handsome, even covered in grime and sweat. Although we've been back home for a few weeks, I can't get over how much more I like him in his ogre form. He was hot as hell as a human but as an ogre... What can I say? I've got a monster kink.

"No, don't go. I just..." I search for words. How can I salvage this moment without ruining it?

I sigh. "I'm pregnant."

"What?" Beck's face blanks, and he drops his sack and rope on the floor.

"And I'm pretty sure it's yours."

"Are you joking?" he asks. His expression is unreadable.

"Well, kind of. I'm actually a hundred percent sure it's yours."

He stalks toward me with an intense stare. Is he angry? I don't even know if he ever wanted kids. The conversation never came up. "Liona?"

I back away from him until I hit the dresser behind me. "I'm not joking. I am pregnant. Well, at least according to Gilda, who might be full of shit. But now that I think about it, it would explain a lot—the vomiting, the mood swings, the tiredness, the more than usual fantastic tits."

He takes his eyes off mine and trails down my body, stopping at my stomach, and reaches out to place his hands on it.

He still hasn't said a word and I can't take it anymore. "So, what are you thinking?"

He looks up at me, his eyes filled with tears.

I think back to the story of how his parents died when he was so young. This must be hard for him. He barely grew up with any parents and now he's being forced into parenthood. Shit. I knew I should have told him in a better way. Do they have therapists in the magical community? Because it sure as shit seems like we're going to need one.

"I just..." He swallows. "I just couldn't believe it was possible to love you anymore, and now here we are and you're giving me a child." He grabs the back of my neck and pulls me in, kissing me with an intensity that curls my toes.

I pull back, unable to suppress the smile on my face. "So, you're excited we're having a baby?"

"Excited? I might have a heart attack my heart's so full!" He leans in to kiss me again. "I love you," he whispers in between kisses.

I kiss him back, wondering what I did to deserve so much love. Damn, life is good.

CHAPTER NINETEEN

Beck

"How do I look?" I stare into the outhouse mirror and brush a strand of hair behind my ear.

"Hot as shit, man," Winston says from behind me.

I turn back and glare at him. "Really?"

"What? You asked."

"You could have just said 'good' like a normal person."

"Well, obviously, I'm not a normal person." He adjusts my black tie and straightens my blazer. "I can tell you're nervous. Everything's going to go great."

I breathe out. He's right. I don't know why I feel like the sky's about to fall but also like I'm about to receive the best present ever. I'm marrying Liona. Everything is going to go fine. She's going to say yes, and we'll live happily ever after. Except knowing her, she'll probably pull some shit. I grin, thinking about her devilish games.

Winston peeks out from the brush surrounding us. "Wow, it's like the whole village is here."

Nerves rush through my bloodstream. "Is everyone here?"

"No, there's no sign of that bastard."

I've told Winston about Donny's attack on Liona. I trust him to help me keep her safe.

"Alright, let's not keep these people waiting. Let's get you married." He slaps my back and gives me a gentle push out towards the end of the aisle at the edge of the clearing.

The second I step out, the quartet of instruments at the front of the aisle begins playing on their own. The crowd looks back at us. Everyone's here. The three blind mice amble around the edge of the seats, using their canes to find an empty spot. The giants scrunch together at the back row, looking utterly ridiculous trying to squat down in the normal-sized seats. Smaller fairies flutter overhead. Sirens have transformed their tails into legs, their scales sparkling in the sunlight. Dragons of all shapes and sizes squish in among the rest. It's almost like one of the board meetings except much livelier.

Winston smiles at me and pats my back again before walking down the aisle by himself. He's wearing a black fitted suit and his hair is gelled back. He waves at the audience members as he descends toward the front, where Mother Nature stands to officiate our ceremony. A string of flowers flows out from around her, covering the aisle.

Then I'm alone with everyone staring at me. I gulp and steal my face. I know I'm supposed to look like the embodiment of happiness and bliss on my wedding day, but I hate being the center of attention. But getting married was my idea. What the fuck is wrong with me?

I march down the aisle, not turning my gaze toward anyone. When I reach the front and stand in front of Winston, he pats my back. I gaze at the ground before me with my fist clenched tight. I'm counting the seconds before this is over.

My attention shifts as the crowd gets to their feet and turns to the front of the aisle. Liona stands in a ray of sunshine, her arm interlocked with Glinda's. She walks towards me, and every nervous thought, all my longing for this ceremony to end, dissipates. The whole crowd dissipates. Suddenly it's just me and her in this clearing, in these woods, and in this world. It's just me and her.

I can't hold back the tears flowing from my eyes. She's so beautiful in her white dress and veil. She's always beautiful, but seeing her like this, with her face alight with a pregnancy glow, I begin to believe in divinity. She's an angel sent from heaven. Who knows why she was sent to a son of a bitch like me, but damn it if I'm not thankful.

After what feels like a lifetime, she makes her way to me. Gilda hands her over and kisses me on the cheek. "Take care of her," she whispers before fluttering to the front row and standing next to another gray-haired woman. My gaze rests on the woman. I know her. It's G.M. Fairy. Why is she here in the magical community? My heart rate quickens, wondering if she's here to reclaim her debt, but G.M. just smiles at us.

Liona squeezes my hand, returning my attention to her; all worries melt away again.

"You may be seated," Mother Nature says as she addresses the crowd. Her trail of flowers has grown on the ground around us, encircling us in blooms.

"You look hot," Liona whispers to me.

"You too," I whisper back.

She shrugs her shoulders. "I know." I want to kiss the smile right off her face.

Mother Nature goes through the marriage semantics, talking about what it means and what we're doing today symbolizes, blah, blah, blah. I barely catch a minute of it because Liona's beauty hypnotizes me. I don't tune in until I hear, "Beck, do you take Liona to be your wife?"

It's silent and all eyes are on me. I don't need to ponder. "I do!" I nearly shout and Liona giggles at my eagerness.

Mother Nature turns her attention to Liona. "Liona, do you take Beck to be your husband?" The crowd is even quieter this time. Liona came to this community as my prisoner. She's a gorgeous woman and I'm a hideous ogre. I bet everyone has an even harder time believing she could love me than I do.

I don't know if it's just me and my nerves, but it seems like Liona hesitates. Like she's mentally weighing her options back and forth. What if this is all a long-con revenge scheme for capturing her a year ago? What if seeing me at the altar and everything it symbolizes makes her question if this is what she wants?

My panic sprawls out and crawls deep inside me. I'm ready to abandon hope until Liona's smile spreads across her face like a sunset appearing after a storm. "Of course I do!" She leans in and I grab her.

"Brat," I whisper before bending her over and kissing her.

She giggles as she kisses me back, her hands running through my hair.

"Okay, I guess you can kiss the bride and I now pronounce you husband and wife," Mother Nature says quickly and laughs.

Oh, yeah. I guess we're supposed to wait. Fuck it.

The crowd stands up, clapping, hollering, and making all the other noises magical creatures can make.

I scoop Liona in my arms and march her down the aisle, not taking my lips away from her until she pulls back and says, "Now what?"

Of course, we've planned a reception with a big feast and dancing, but that can wait. "Oh, I have big plans for you, Mrs. Ogre."

I can tell she knows what I mean by how her cheeks heat. "Don't you think they'll miss us if we're gone too long?"

"Like you care."

She laughs. "You're right." She starts at my shirt buttons.

I pick up my speed, running through the forest to a place we'll be unheard—well, for the most part. I stop at a clearing and lean Liona against a tree, moving my hands over her body. A thought pops into my head, and I pull back. "Are you happy?"

She furrows her brows and searches my face. "Of course, but...."

"But, what?"

"I'll be a hell of a lot happier once I have you inside of me."

"You're wish is my command."

And just like that, we're in our happily ever after. Who knew a monster like me could get so lucky?

Epilogue

WINSTON - ONE YEAR LATER

"Did you see this?" Liona flings a newspaper onto my desk.

It takes my brain a second to switch from crunching numbers to recognizing what she's put in front of me. I pick it up and scan the title of the front page story. "Lawrence and Victoria Farque, Heirs of the Dual-Lock Home Security Empire, Arrested for Espionage."

I glance up at Liona, who has a giddy smile plastered on her face. I scan the rest of the article as she summarizes it for me. "Basically, after I made Lawrence release all the evidence of his and Victoria's relationship, the public was concerned that the footage looked to be taken from security systems. They filed an investigation and found that Lawrence and the whole company were storing footage of people without their knowledge. They just went to trial and lost. Apparently, Lawrence's big lawyers couldn't help." She's practically beaming with pleasure.

I slap the paper down. "Look at that! Your moment of rage saved the day!" I stand up to hug her.

"I'd been wondering why they haven't come after us, but this explains it." She breathes out and looks around the office. Her beaming expression switches to concern. "How long have you been here?"

I sit on the edge of my desk. My collar is unbuttoned, and my sleeves are rolled up. I haven't looked in the mirror in a few hours, but I probably look like shit. I feel like shit and my office matches the sentiment. "G.M. is coming tonight. I have to make sure everything's perfect." I don't want to reveal that I've actually been here for ten hours straight.

"Winston, she's been here plenty of times. The club is doing great. She's going to love it."

"She's only ever been here before and during the opening. Now that we're in the full swing of things, it feels like more pressure." I turn back to the papers on my desk and flip through them.

Liona grabs my arm. "Winston, the club opens in less than an hour. You have to get ready before people start showing up. Let me know what you need, and I'll take care of it."

I smile at her. She's a good friend. She's also part owner of this club, but I'm the manager, so all day-to-day tasks go to me.

I shake my head. "No, it's okay. I'm done. I'll get ready. Just make sure you and Beck are ready for your performance tonight. How are you feeling about it?"

She sighs and brushes her hair behind her ears. She's wearing a black leather skirt with a black tank top. I can tell she's ready to perform. "I'm excited but nervous. This is our first time back on stage since having the baby."

"Well, you look great. I know that G.M. Fairy is looking forward to you both tonight."

She rolls her eyes. "Thanks. I don't know why she likes us so much. I still can't get over the fact that her payment for the Charming Potion was for Beck and me to perform and then for us to help her open another Happily Ever Endings here in the community. It almost seems too good to be true."

I shrug. "You and Beck are special, and she can see that. Besides, this is a good business opportunity for her. We're making her a lot of money."

She shoves my shoulder. "See, that's the way you need to be thinking about her coming in tonight. There's no need to be nervous."

"You're right." I stand up and start collecting my bag to change and get ready.

"Have you ever thought about performing? You know, actually, participating instead of just watching? I know I'd love to see you up on that stage."

She doesn't mean it as a jab, but it stings. She doesn't know how badly I wish to be part of something, to have a real connection with someone, even if it's just physical. But it isn't possible, and I'm not ready to explain, even to one of my best friends. I steel my face, not wanting to let my true emotions show, and turn to her. "You know me. I'd rather watch."

She smiles and shakes her head before turning to the door. "Whatever floats your boat!"

"Oh, wait!" I call before Liona exits my office. "Did you check on that shipment?"

"Oh yeah. It didn't come and we're out."

"No! Not the Gumdrop Buttons!" I rub my temples.

"It's fine! People will have a good enough time without them. I know I sure as hell don't need them." She gives me a wink before heading out the door.

I sigh and roll my shoulders before walking to the mirror in the corner of my office. Man, I look like shit. My hair is an unruly mess, sticking up from all angles. My blue eyes are darkened by the bags under them and there are coffee stains all over my shirt. I check my watch. Shit, I only have forty more minutes until the club opens. I head towards the bathroom at the far end of my office. I know a hot shower will clear my head and make me look a hell of a lot better.

***

"Winston, darling, it's so good to see you." G.M. Fairy flutters over to me and air kisses both of my cheeks. She's wearing a bejeweled red dress, and behind her is her entourage. All I can see is the tall trolls that flank both sides of her, their expressions hidden by their dark shades, but I know she has more people behind them. She always comes with a crew.

"You look ravishing as always, Ms. Fairy." I kiss her hand delicately.

"That's why I love you, Winston. You're always a devilish flirt. How's everything going?"

I turn towards the club. "See for yourself." The night is in full swing. The music is a low growl. The lights are dim but bright enough to reveal the most intimate scenes. It's packed; creatures of all sorts walk around and lounge on every surface. A performance is happening on the main stage—a solo act with one of the communities' sirens.

When G.M. Fairy proposed opening this club here in the magical community on the night of Liona and Beck's wedding, I thought it was a stupid idea. Our community is small, with only about three thousand members. I wasn't even sure if most would be interested in something like this. But G.M. assured me that creatures would come from near and far, and she thought our community had a little more spunk than I thought. She was right. There were people I knew my whole life who I never even thought had sex that were regulars. It was a community hit and a frequent stop for all magical creatures visiting the Florida area. Sure, we had to figure out some border control issues and who not to let in, but it didn't take long for me to develop a potion that only allowed magical beings into the community.

The club had given me a new purpose and made me feel part of something greater. It also helped satisfy my most primal needs. The ones I couldn't satisfy on my own. No, it never got rid of the longing I knew I'd never be able to extinguish, but it keeps those real needs at bay.

G.M. nods as she looks around. "Everything looks great. Great job, Winston. Are Liona and Beck here?"

"Yes. They're just getting ready for their performance."

"Ah, I can't wait to see. I hear that after a baby, everything is heightened. I want to talk to them before they go on. Can you direct me to their dressing room?"

"Yes, of course."

I begin to lead the way, but she stops me. "Oh, before I forget. I brought someone for you."

"For me?" I look back at the crowd of people behind her, still unable to see much due to the towering trolls.

"Yes, I figured that you might be able to help her. She has a condition similar to yours, well, sort of."

G.M. Fairy is one of the only people that know the real me. That's how we met so many years ago. I came to her to seek help. Unfortunately, she couldn't do much and it was my sole cross to bear, but I've learned how to live through it and for now, that's enough.

"Marigold, darling, come here," she calls back to her entourage.

The crowd parts, and a small woman walks through them.

My heart stops.

I've always been keen on the beauty around me. I've never been one to deny myself the simple pleasure of gazing upon a beautiful woman, but this feeling rushing through me is different.

Marigold walks next to G.M., her face hung low. She's wearing white silk gloves. I can imagine why.

"Marigold, I'd like to introduce you to Winston."

She looks up at me and if I thought my world stopped before, I was gravely mistaken. Her hazel eyes seem to take inventory of every piece of me. She tucks a strand of her golden blonde hair behind her ear. Her cheeks heat when she catches my stare, and she returns her gaze down to the floor.

The disappearance of her gaze on me feels like air has been taken from my lungs. I want to grab her face and demand she returns her eyes to me, but I don't, I just bow. "It's a pleasure to meet you, Marigold." I don't reach to take her hand. I know that wouldn't be a good idea. But every cell in my body begs to touch her, to grab her and never let go. And then the realization of G.M. Fairy's words ring through me, *"She has a condition similar to yours,"* and a weight falls on my chest. The realization that she can never be mine—never be in my arms. I've known her for two seconds, but it's enough. These two seconds are all it takes for the girl I can never have to consume all of me.

Read Winston's Story, Spellbound Seduction: A Wizard Love Story

Thanks For Reading!

Thank you for reading! If you liked *Stay In My Swamp: Happily Ever After*, please make sure to leave a review on Amazon and Goodreads.

Want more of G.M. Fairy? Check out her next books...

Spellbound Seduction: A Wizard Love Story

Book 3 and Standalone: Winston the Wizard is a master of magic but a stranger to love. He's lived a full life in the hidden world of the magical community but lives with a condition that makes it impossible to connect fully. He's content with his life as the manager of Happily Ever Endings, a club for adult enchantments, until he meets Marigold— a young woman who suffers from a similar condition, and she needs his help to cope with it. Winston feels an instant connection with her but knows they can never be. Can he overcome his fears and help her find happiness? Or will he lose her to the curse that haunts them both? Find out in this spellbinding romance of magic and mystery.

My AI: A Robot Why-Choose Love Story

After social media star Azzy, has a very public panic attack at a red-carpeted award show, her best friend orders her an Andro Corp. Bodyguard. When her robot bodyguard gets delivered, Azzy quickly realizes Model REM082 is the man of her dreams. Things start heating up as Remmy, as she likes to call him, becomes more and more sentient and does whatever it takes to please her.

Stay up to date on all things G.M. Fairy....

Made in the USA
Thornton, CO
10/18/23 22:10:55

187eeb2d-b1de-42ad-b5c3-b9fa76f40cc4R01